Lone Star Daddy

STELLA BAGWELL

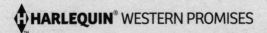

Recycling programs
for this product may
not exist in your area.

ISBN-13: 978-0-373-00362-4

Lone Star Daddy

Printed in U.S.A.

After writing more than eighty books for Harlequin, **Stella Bagwell** still finds it exciting to create new stories and bring her characters to life. She loves all things Western and has been married to her own real cowboy for forty-four years. Living on the south Texas coast, she also enjoys being outdoors and helping her husband care for the horses, cats and dog that call their small ranch home. The couple has one son, who teaches high school mathematics and is also an athletic director. Stella loves hearing from readers. They can contact her at stellabagwell@gmail.com.

Books by Stella Bagwell

Harlequin Special Edition

Men of the West
Daddy Wore Spurs
The Lawman's Noelle
Wearing the Rancher's Ring
One Tall, Dusty Cowboy
A Daddy for Dillon
The Baby Truth
The Doctor's Calling
His Texas Baby
Christmas with the Mustang Man
His Medicine Woman
Daddy's Double Duty
His Texas Wildflower
The Deputy's Lost and Found
Branded with His Baby
Lone Star Daddy

Montana Mavericks: Striking It Rich
Paging Dr. Right

The Fortunes of Texas
The Heiress and the Sheriff

Visit the Author Profile page at Harlequin.com for more titles.

To Spider John,
I love you, my boy.

Chapter One

The woman was definitely pregnant, Jonas Redman decided, and from the looks of her she could go into labor any day! Quint had told him that his sister, Alexa, was a young, single woman and that she was expecting. But the man hadn't mentioned that the baby would be arriving so soon.

Jonas's initial reaction was to turn tail and head straight back to Texas. Unfortunately, he wasn't in a position to leave the Chaparral. The desert mountain ranch was going to be his home for as long as it took to complete the job. A job that had nothing to do with raising cattle and horses.

In a steady gait, he walked across the lawn to intercept her. "Ms. Cantrell?" he called out as she neared the front steps of the huge hacienda-style house. "Could I speak with you for a minute?"

Pausing on the neatly clipped grass, Alexa Cantrell turned toward the voice and watched with faint surprise as a tall man, wearing faded denim and a black cowboy hat, approached her. Normally, the working hands on the Chaparral Ranch didn't need to come by the house. But then, she'd not been living here for the past five years, so maybe things had changed.

Or maybe this wasn't an ordinary ranch hand, Alexa thought, as he came to a stop a few steps away. He certainly didn't look ordinary. He was tall and lean, with sun-browned skin, wide, strong shoulders and authority stamped all over his rugged features. The brim of his hat shaded his eyes, but she could see a pair of thick brown brows and sun lines fanning from the corners. Sandy-brown hair lay in unruly waves about his ears and the back of his neck.

"Yes. May I help you with something?" she asked politely.

Moving forward, he extended his hand to

her. "I'm Jonas Redman, the ranch's new general manager. I happened to see you waving your mother off a moment ago and thought I'd take the opportunity to introduce myself."

So this was the man taking her brother's place, Alexa thought. She clasped her hand around his and was instantly aware of rough, callused skin and warmth that radiated right through her palm.

"It's nice to meet you, Mr. Redman. Quint has spoken of you. He warned me that you'd be coming around if you ran into trouble."

His eyes, which she could now see were a hazel green, narrowed a fraction more.

"Warned you? Sounds like he's already expecting me to fall short."

Alexa laughed softly. "I'm sorry. I guess I chose the wrong word. He only told me that you'd be coming to me if there was a decision you weren't comfortable making on your own. Does that sound better?"

A corner of his chiseled mouth turned slightly upward, and Alexa was shocked to find herself mesmerized by his features. Somewhere between thirty-five and forty, he was not a pretty boy. In fact, his appearance couldn't have been more opposite to that of the father of the baby growing inside her.

Jonas Redman was the epitome of toughness. A man with muscles honed from working with his back and hands, a man who often lifted his face to the sun and wiped sweat from his brow.

Her comment eased the tense lines on his face. "Yes. That'll do fine, ma'am."

His voice was low and raspy, with a twang that told Alexa he wasn't a New Mexican native. Interest about the man sparked within, shocking her with its appearance. She hadn't looked twice at a man since—well, since Barry had charmed his way into her life.

Gesturing toward the porch, she said, "Would you like to have a cup of coffee or a glass of lemonade? Mother and I just had something before she left."

He glanced over his shoulder, toward a portion of the working ranch yard. Even though the nearest barn was more than a hundred yards away, the few trees scattered between didn't block the view.

"I suppose I could take five minutes," he said. "It doesn't appear the men have arrived back from the west pasture yet."

Nodding, she started toward the house, and he fell into step beside her.

"You're not from around here, are you?"

she questioned as they climbed the two wide steps to the porch.

"Texas, ma'am. I used to live near San Antonio. But I decided to migrate west."

"Oh? You didn't like it there?"

"I must have liked it," he answered. "Up until three weeks ago I'd always lived in Texas. But I guess I got the itch to see something new."

By now they were on the long, concrete porch connected to a huge, cream-colored stucco house trimmed with dark wooden shutters and doors. Above their heads, a balcony served as a roof for the porch and a sunning spot for the rooms on the second floor of the structure.

Three weeks ago, when Jonas had first arrived, Quint had given him a brief tour of the house. The structure was big enough for a simple man like him to get lost in. Which was probably good, since it looked as though he was going to have to spend time in it with this woman.

"Well, I hope you like it here," the young woman said. "Our grandfather has Quint so tied up developing land near Capitan that he hardly has time to telephone. I know my brother is very relieved to have you taking care of things now that he's working on other projects."

"Your brother is an easy man to please."

She gestured for him to take a seat on one of the willow chairs grouped together at the east end of the porch. Jonas waited for her to ease onto one of the padded cushions before he seated himself. In front of her was a low table with a tray holding glasses, cups and two insulated thermoses.

Leaning forward, she asked, "Coffee or lemonade?"

"The coffee would be nice."

He watched as she poured the hot brown liquid into a bright yellow mug. Her hands were long and slender, as were her arms and legs. Even with her very pregnant belly, Quint could see that normally she was a shapely woman. As for her facial features, she looked nothing like her brother. In fact, she didn't resemble any woman he'd seen before. Her face was square shaped, her mouth wide. Eyes the color of a robin's egg were set beneath a pair of winged black brows. Prominent cheekbones slanted upward toward her temples, giving her a regal, almost exotic appearance. In spite of himself, he felt his gaze drawn to her comely face.

"Cream or sugar?"

Jonas released a breath of air that had backed up in his throat. "No. Black is good."

She handed him the mug and he murmured his thanks.

"So how are you settling in?" she asked. "Having any problems with the men?"

Jonas swallowed a sip of coffee before he answered. "No problems. I've had a bit of time to get to know all the hands, and they all seem to be well acquainted with their jobs. Quint tells me that most of them have worked here for years."

"That's right," she agreed. "We don't have much of a turnover. We try to keep the men's salaries and benefits comparable to others in the area, and thankfully, most of them are content to stay."

When Jonas had first approached Alexa Cantrell, he'd not intended for the meeting to turn into a friendly visit. He was on a mission, and normally it was his style to keep things on a business track. But this was a time when he couldn't behave in his normal fashion. If he did, it would only raise this woman's eyebrows, and the less he did that, the better off they'd all be.

Resting his mug on his knee, he darted a

glance at her. She was a young and lovely woman. Why wasn't there a wedding band on her finger? A man at her side, eager and waiting to become a father?

Maybe there is, Jonas. Maybe Alexa Cantrell is one of those progressive women who doesn't necessarily want a traditional family. Maybe the baby's father is still hanging close. Still her lover.

Clearing his throat, he said, "I hear Mrs. Cantrell is going to be gone for nearly a month."

"That's right. She just left to catch her plane. She's visiting my half brothers in South Texas."

Jonas forced himself to take another sip of coffee, as though he was enjoying the break, as though every nerve in his body wasn't wound as tight as a cornered mustang.

"So that leaves you alone in the house."

Her brow puckered with confusion and Jonas felt like kicking himself. He was going at this all wrong. But then, he'd never been known for finesse. When there was a job to be done he jumped in with both feet. With a fight to be fought, he leaped in with two fists.

"I don't mean to sound rude, Mr. Redman, but what are you asking?"

"Uh—seems your brother has asked me to look out for you while your mother is away. He wants me to move into the house with you."

She didn't try to hide her shock as she stared at him. "What? Is this some sort of joke?"

Jonas wished it were. He had too much on his mind, too much to do in a short time without having to deal with a pregnant woman. But Quint had been understanding enough to permit him to take over the position of general manager of the Chaparral. And being on this huge ranch allowed him access to information he would otherwise have to spend days digging for.

"I'm sorry. This is not anything to joke about. Your brother was concerned about your safety. I promised him I would remain in the house at night—just to alleviate his fears."

She drew her shoulders back and at the same time rested a hand on the upper part of her belly. Jonas couldn't help but wonder if she'd already been told the sex of the baby. And when was it due? He didn't know much at all about expecting women, but this one didn't look that far away from giving birth, and that left him a little more than uneasy.

"I'm sorry, too. Because my brother doesn't run my life. I do. And I hardly need a night nurse."

Jonas couldn't stop a wry smile from twisting his lips. "Maybe you'd better take another look at me, Ms. Cantrell. I'm about as far away from a nurse as you can get."

Her square jaw tightened further, and Jonas got the impression that if pushed, she could be more than stubborn.

"All right," she said curtly. "Let me phrase it this way. I don't need a bodyguard."

"I wouldn't label me one of those either. I'm just a cowboy. And your brother is simply concerned."

She breathed deeply, and Jonas watched her nostrils flare like those of a mare getting ready to kick with both hind feet.

"Overly so, it seems. And for your information, Sassy, our maid lives in the house. I won't be alone."

She'd not bothered to serve herself a drink, and Jonas decided this meeting had moved far beyond sharing refreshments. "From what Quint says, Sassy is young and always on the go. Especially at night. He wants a man in the house just in case there's a problem."

"I think the problem is him," she muttered under her breath.

Jonas bit back his frustration. "I'm sorry the idea of me staying with you is so upsetting. Tell you what. You talk it over with your brother. As far as I'm concerned, I'm very comfortable in the bunkhouse. And maybe you have a male friend or relative that you'd rather have stay with you." Rising to his feet, he placed the remainder of his coffee on the low table. "I'd better get back to work, Ms. Cantrell. It was nice meeting you. And thanks for the coffee."

He was starting to walk off the porch when she suddenly called out to him. "Wait a minute, Mr. Redman. Please."

Slowly she rose to her feet, and he paused near the steps as she walked over to him. As she did, a faint breeze ruffled her black hair and teased it around her shoulders. Earlier he'd caught the scent of honeysuckle emanating from her, and as she drew near, the sweet perfume intensified, reminding him of home.

He remained silent and simply waited for her to explain.

She shook her head slightly. "Look, I hope

you won't take this personally, but I'm perfectly capable of looking after myself."

"You're going to have a baby soon."

"That doesn't make me an invalid."

He lifted the hat from his head and ran a hand through the flattened waves. "No. It makes you vulnerable," he said as he settled the Stetson back into place.

She momentarily closed her eyes, and in that moment Jonas realized just how much her blue eyes dominated her features. They were as fresh and cool as the New Mexico sky and just as enchanting.

"I have a phone with me at all times," she reasoned. "If I go into early labor, all I have to do is make a call."

"That's good. I'm glad you think I'm not needed. Because frankly, Ms. Cantrell, my hands are full with other duties right now. I've only been here three weeks, and your brother has big plans for this place—plans that I'm only starting to put into motion."

In other words, he didn't want to stay in the ranch house any more than she wanted him to, Alexa thought. That fact should have reassured her. Yet for some ridiculous reason she felt insulted. Men had never dismissed her. Even her failed relationship with Barry had ended because she'd chosen to end it. Not the other way around. The idea that Jonas Redman was simply going to walk away without a backward glance irked her in a way that took her by surprise.

Propping a hand on one hip, she cocked her head to one side. "So you're not going to be moving into the house?"

He smiled a cool little smile, which prickled Alexa's skin. The man was sexy and tough all rolled together. He was also just a tad too independent for her taste. What in the world had Quint been thinking when he'd hired this man; when he'd suggested this long, tall Texan move into the house with her? Had her brother gone crazy?

"No. Not unless you invite me to. Good day, Ms. Cantrell."

Tipping his hat to her, he walked off the porch and toward the barn.

Feeling rather dazed, Alexa leaned against a wooden beam and watched as the man made his way across the ranch yard. The lack of rain had left the ground like powder, and dust rose in little puffs around his black boots. His strides were long and authoritative, their aim directed straight at the cattle barn.

She watched until he disappeared into an

open door, while realizing with a sharp little sting that he'd never once looked back at her, the house or anything behind him.

Maybe he's a man who never looks back, Alexa. Or maybe he considers you at the bottom of his important list.

Irked by the mocking voice in her head, she turned and hurried over to the chair where she'd been sitting. A cell phone was lying next to the tray of refreshments, and after quickly snatching it from the table, she sat down and punched in her brother's number.

After several rings, the voice mail came on. Alexa snapped the phone shut and leaned her head against the back of the chair.

For one split second she felt like crying. But she bit her lip and pushed away the emotional storm. She'd never been a weak woman, and she wasn't about to start just because her hormones were in overdrive.

Damn it. Things in her family had been in turmoil for the past several months. Why had Quint finally caved in to their grandfather and gone off to work on another section of Apache Wells? Now wasn't a good time. Not with their mother gallivanting off to Texas and Alexa getting nearer and nearer to the birth of her baby!

Closing her eyes with shame, she pinched the bridge of her nose. What was the matter with her? This selfish attitude wasn't really her. She was grateful that Frankie, their mother, was finally healthy and that she was going to spend time with Mac and Ripp, Alexa's half brothers. After all these years her mother deserved this visit and more. As for Quint, he had his hands full. Especially this past year and a half, since their father, Lewis, had died and Abe, their grandfather, was placing more and more demands on him. Alexa didn't need to be adding to her brother's problems. She needed to be helping him in every way that she could. And she knew they wanted everything in order so they would be here to support her when the baby came.

That thought had just entered her head when the phone in her lap rang. Picking it up, she saw that it was Quint and she quickly answered. "Hello, big brother."

"Just returning your call," he replied. "Is everything okay there?"

She paused as she tried to decide exactly what to tell him. "Sure. Everything is fine. I was just touching base with you, that's all. Did I catch you at a busy time?"

He sighed. "I've finally gotten the builders out here to start on the stables, but they're missing some of the material they need. I'll have to drive down to Ruidoso and put in an order."

"You can't do it over the phone?"

"No. It's some things I need to look over and okay first."

"Well, Mother got off a few minutes ago," she informed him.

"Good. You can't know how happy I am about this trip of hers. What about you?"

"Sure I'm happy for her. And she's promised to be back at least two weeks before the baby is due."

At first, when Alexa had learned that her mother had been keeping a past life secret from them and that Frankie also had two sons living in Texas, she'd been shocked and a little angry. All these years, Alexa had never imagined Frankie as anything more than a wife to Lewis, a mother to her and Quint. Learning that their mother had abandoned a family prior to theirs had shaken Alexa more than she'd ever wanted to admit to herself or anyone.

Quint said, "Getting her sons back in her life has changed Mom for the better."

Alexa swallowed at the lump that had suddenly lodged in her throat. Barry had turned out to be someone very different than the man she'd initially believed him to be. And then she'd learned that her mother was someone different, too. All of it together had been difficult for Alexa to deal with. Yet Quint seemed to be taking everything in stride. He was excited at having two older brothers and couldn't wait to get them out here for an extended visit.

"Seems that way," Alexa murmured, then drawing in a breath, added, "I met the new manager, Mr. Redman, a few minutes ago."

There was a long pause before Quint finally replied. "Oh. How did that go? Please don't tell me you got crosswise with the man. I can't deal with that, Alexa. Not right now."

She stiffened her spine. Did everyone view her as difficult? Now that she was home again, was her brother expecting her to be a problem rather than a help? The idea cut right through her. True, she'd shown up here at the ranch unexpectedly, throwing kinks in the plans her mother and brother had already made. But she'd wanted to surprise them. She'd not stopped to think that they had lives and schedules that didn't always include her.

"No. No problems. He seems competent enough." Now where had that come from? she wondered with self-disgust. She and Jonas Redman hadn't discussed anything about the ranch or how to run it. But then, was it really her place to say how the Chaparral should be operated? For the past five years she'd chosen to stay away from her home and live in Santa Fe. At that time, she'd believed that living in the city would bring the change she needed in her life. She'd thought being Senator Hutchins's aide would be the beginning of a satisfying career that would keep her away from the ranch. She'd not counted on Barry or the baby happening. Now her life felt as though it had splintered in all directions, and not one was the right one for her.

She pushed back a sigh as her brother began to speak.

"Jonas is more than competent, Alexa. We're very fortunate to get him." The phone crackled, telling Alexa her brother must be driving through the mountains, causing the signal to break. "I—you were—with him staying in the house. He—but I—made him see how important it was—have you safe."

Alexa wearily wiped a hand over her eyes.

"Your phone is breaking up, Quint. Everything is fine here. I'll talk to you later."

After putting away the phone, she reached for the tray of refreshments and carried it into the house. The dimly lit interior was cool as Alexa made her way through rooms with low ceilings, whitewashed walls, and comfortable Western furnishings. A large kitchen was located on the bottom floor at the back of the house. When she stepped into the room, she found the ranch's longtime cook watering potted succulents rowed along a windowsill.

The sound of Alexa's footsteps tapping against the tile floor announced her arrival, and the woman turned just as Alexa placed the tray of refreshments down on the cabinet counter.

"Alexa! You shouldn't have carried that heavy tray!" she scolded. "Why didn't you call me?"

Alexa smiled at the woman. Reena Crow had been working for the Cantrells even before Alexa was born. She was now in her mid-fifties but looked at least ten years younger. She was petite and slender, and her shoulder-length hair was as straight as a stick and salt-and-pepper in color. Her brown skin implied a Native American ancestry, but her pale green eyes belied it.

At the age of eighteen, Reena had come to work on the Chaparral as a maid, but after a few years her culinary skills had pushed her to the position of cook. Now widowed and with a grown daughter living away, Reena spent her days on the ranch and her nights taking care of her ninety-year-old mother.

"It wasn't that heavy, Reena. I think both thermoses are practically empty," Alexa said as she began placing dirty glasses and mugs in the sink.

"So Frankie is already gone?"

Alexa bit back a sigh. She'd come home, eager to help with stacks of bookkeeping for the Chaparral while her mother was away. She'd not envisioned having to deal with a man like Jonas Redman in the house.

You can always tell him no thanks, Alexa. You can flatly refuse to allow him in the house.

Yes, she could refuse, Alexa thought glumly. But that would only throw more worry onto Quint. And she already felt guilty enough about the heavy load her brother carried. Besides, now that she thought about it, she'd overreacted to the whole thing. Jonas Redman wasn't going to intrude on her life. Even if he was one of the sexiest men she'd ever laid eyes on, his interests obviously didn't include a very pregnant single woman. And she'd be incredibly conceited to think otherwise.

"Yes. I waved her off a few minutes ago."

"She's very excited," Reena said. "And happy. That's so good to see. Earlier this winter I was afraid she was going to die."

"So was I, Reena. But once she realized she had something to live for, she agreed to the heart operation, which she desperately needed. Thank God."

Reena climbed down from the step chair and put her watering can to one side. "Well, you having this baby has also done wonders for her." She slanted a concerned eye at Alexa. "Are you feeling okay? Your face is flushed."

No doubt, Alexa thought wryly. Jonas Redman had stirred her blood. Although she wasn't sure why. He'd simply been following orders. And he'd not given her one sly look, one suggestive word. Yet she'd found herself having thoughts about him that were disturbing. She'd never reacted to any other man like that before she was pregnant.

"I'm fine. It's just a little warm out this afternoon."

Alexa began to fill the sink with warm water, but Reena quickly elbowed her away.

"Go. Rest. Do something. I'll tend to these."

Knowing better than to argue with the woman, Alexa left the kitchen and climbed the stairs. Earlier this morning, before she'd left her bedroom, she'd opened the heavy wooden door that led onto the balcony, and now a cool breeze wafted through the large room and rustled the bed skirt on the dark oak four-poster.

These days she tired easily, and oftentimes her body begged for a nap. But this afternoon she was too wired to think about sleep and ignoring the bed, she walked out onto the balcony.

The ranch house sat in a valley that ran for several miles between pine-covered mountains. To the right she could see the Rio Bonito meandering through banks lined with willows and aspens. To the left, a massive ranch yard with barns, sheds, outbuildings and cattle pens spread across many acres.

In all her life and all her travels, Alexa had never seen a prettier place than the Chaparral. And from her father she'd inherited a deep love of the land. Yet at the moment she took no solace in the majestic landscape sweeping southwest toward Alto. No, her thoughts were on Jonas Redman and the fact that she was now going to have to go over to the ranch yard and tell him that she'd changed her mind about having him for a housemate.

Across from the house, at the end of a long line of horse stables, Jonas stood in his office with a cell phone jammed to his ear while Captain Leo Weaver with the Texas Rangers tossed questions at him.

"How much longer do you think this is going to take, Jonas?"

Frowning, Jonas peered out the dusty window as he watched a couple of cowboys attempt to repair a wooden feed trough with hammer and nails. "Right now it's impossible to say, Captain. I've seen nothing moving on this property or the surrounding property. But these ranches around here are hardly small. I actually need another man here—an extra set of eyes and ears. As it stands, it's going to take me days more riding to search out the backside of this ranch."

Normally the Rangers didn't go out of their jurisdiction, which was the state of Texas. But this was a bistate crime, and New Mexico had invited them and asked for their help. As a result, Jonas had been chosen for the job.

"What about using a four-wheeler? That ought to speed things up."

"Most places are far too rough for an ATV. Horse or mule is the safest means of searching. That's why another man would sure help."

"Right now I don't have a spare man to put on the case. Besides, two Rangers would be easier to spot than one. Another new hand coming onto the ranch—especially one that isn't from the area—would make everyone suspicious. You're gonna have to go this one alone, Jonas."

Jonas bit back the frustration he was feeling. Leo was right; two new outsiders coming to work on the Chaparral at the same time could throw up red flags. His captain expected him to deal with the matter on his own, and Jonas would. It would just take him a lot longer. And he wanted to be gone from this place. He wanted to go home to Texas. And he damned sure didn't want to babysit a pregnant woman.

"Yeah," he muttered.

"The Cattlemen's Association and the state livestock regulators are on me about this, Jonas. They're worried about diseases being shipped in and spreading through healthy herds. We're talking millions of dollars at stake. Not to mention the criminal aspect of it. Mexico does not want to give up its corner on the Corriente cattle market and Texas does not want Mexican cattle shipped illegally across its borders. Presently, all the information points to rustlers routing their stock through southern New Mexico. Particularly from your point through Portales and Clovis. And all of the areas—Texas, Mexico and New Mexico are working on it. But we think you are in the right area to uncover something. Have you picked up on anything at all?"

"Not much. Right now I'm just trying to look like a ranch manager and get a sense of the personal routines of the hands."

"You think one of them is in on it?"

Jonas suddenly straightened his shoulder away from the window when he spotted Alexa Cantrell walking slowly across the dusty ground toward his office. She'd changed from the slacks and blouse she'd been wearing earlier into a blue-and-white flowered dress with a peasant neckline. The wind caused the hem to dance around her shapely calves and mold against her mounded stomach. He'd never realized a woman could be pregnant and sexy at the same time. Until now.

"Hard to say, Captain. Some people are more difficult to read than others. And some don't talk about anything. I'm hoping something will break soon."

"Let me know the minute it does."

As Alexa neared the door of the office, Jonas lowered his voice. "Will do. Someone's coming—I'd better get off."

He snapped the phone together and dropped it into his shirt pocket just as the woman stepped through the door. She stared at the empty desk chair, then jerked her head sideways as she realized he was standing a few steps away from her.

"Oh. There you are."

Jonas stepped away from the window to greet her. "This is a surprise. I wasn't expecting to see you again today."

Folding her hands in front of her, she turned to face him. There was a humble look to her face, which he'd not detected earlier, and he could only wonder what had brought about the change. But then, he knew from experience that it didn't take much to swing a woman's mood.

"Am I interrupting anything?"

Nothing that she could know about, he thought grimly. Only Quint knew he was a Texas Ranger, and only Quint knew his reason for being on the ranch. Perhaps things might reach a point in the future where he would be forced to reveal himself to Alexa. But for the present, the less she knew, the safer they would all be. Nothing he did should bring danger to the family. He'd continue to ensure that.

"No. I just stepped into the office to see about ordering a shipment of vaccines for the cattle. Quint says the herd in the west pasture is due to be worked."

She held her palms up in a helpless gesture. "I wish I could tell you more of the ranch's schedule. But I've not been living here for the past five years. In fact, my family wasn't expecting me to move back. I surprised them."

"Yes. Your brother mentioned last week that you suddenly decided to move back from Santa Fe," Jonas informed her as he strode over to an old schoolteacher's desk made of metal and Formica. Propping one hip on the corner, he gestured for her to take the chair in front of him. "Please sit. Hopefully the seat's not too dusty."

She eased gracefully onto the wooden chair, then carefully smoothed her dress over her knees. Without bothering to look at him, she said in a quiet voice, "Well, I'm sure you must have guessed why I'm here."

Looking at her jolted him. Something about her reminded him of just how long he'd lived alone, of how long it had been since he'd imagined having children of his own.

Tucking away all emotion, he said, "Actually, I haven't. Do you have a question for me? A problem?"

"No problem. Unless—" she lifted her face and looked at him "—you've changed your mind about staying in the house with me."

Her voice was stiff and halting, telling Jonas it must have cost her to come to him like this. He almost felt sorry for her. But just almost. He couldn't warm up to people with superior attitudes, and that included beautiful women.

"Why would I change my mind? When I'm given an order, I'm not in a position to change my mind." He tried to smile, but his lips felt uncomfortable as they stretched against his teeth. Smiling was foreign to Jonas, and when he did smile it was usually for effect, not a reflexive action. "Look, Ms. Cantrell, I don't know what's going on in that pretty head of yours. Maybe you just don't like cowhands like me. Maybe they're just a bit beneath your style to have one sleeping in the same house with you. I don't know—I've only met you. But you can rest assured that I consider you a job and nothing more. Now, if you want me to stay in the house, fine. If you don't, that's fine, too."

She didn't blink as he talked, but he did notice that her eyes darkened and her lips folded together.

"You don't have to be insulting about it," she said.

He shrugged. "You didn't have to be, either. But you were."

Her head dropped, and she absently plucked at the soft fabric covering her belly. "Yes, I suppose I was a bit rude," she admitted lowly. "And I'm sorry for that. And I… want to say—my attitude had nothing to do with you personally. I've not been myself here lately. For obvious reasons."

Jonas quietly studied her bent head as all sorts of questions drifted through his mind. The father. Her health. Her plans.

"When is your baby due?"

She lifted her head and looked at him with faint surprise. As though she'd not expected him to consider her personal plight.

"Six weeks from tomorrow."

"Are you doing okay?"

A wry grimace twisted her lips. "You mean, as an unwed mother?"

He slanted an impatient look at her. "That's not what I meant. I'm asking about your health."

Pink color swept across her cheeks. "Sorry. I don't know why I'm being so—defensive."

She thrust a hand through her black hair, then pushed to her feet. Jonas watched curiously as she began to meander around the stark, dusty room while he waited for her to say more.

"My life has been uprooted, and now that my mother and brother are gone, I feel...sort of lost, I suppose. I can't ever remember a time I was on the ranch without any family around. You mentioned that I might ask a male friend or relative to stay with me. Well, I don't have any male friends—not around here. And the only relative is my grandfather Abe, and you'd have to place several sticks of dynamite beneath him to get him to leave his home for any reason."

His gaze took in the proud angle of her head. "From what you say, you've been living away from your family for several years now. You should be used to not having them around."

Pausing at one of the narrow windows, she glanced over her shoulder at him. "You don't miss anything, do you?"

It was his job not to miss anything, he thought. But she couldn't know that. "I'm an outsider, Ms. Cantrell. It's easy for me to look at things logically."

She sighed and turned her gaze back to the windowpane. "You're right. I have lived for five years without seeing my family on a daily basis. But that was in Santa Fe. This is here and now. I'm not used to being on the ranch alone," she reasoned. "I need time to reacquaint myself with everything."

This time the smile on his face came easier. "Have you stopped to think that your brother already understood you might feel that way? Maybe that's why he didn't want you to be alone in that huge house while he and your mother are away."

She reached up and passed a hand across

her forehead, and Jonas thought he could see a tremble to her fingers. Clearly the woman wasn't as independent as she'd first wanted him to believe, and the idea that she was willing to admit that she needed someone was all it took to soften him.

Smiling gently, she turned to face him. "Yes, I suppose he did."

She strode over to where he sat propped on the edge of the desk and extended her hand. "Shall we start over? I'm Alexa Cantrell. Please call me Alexa."

He enfolded her soft little hand in his and felt his heart thump in a way that practically startled him. "All right, Alexa," he said huskily. "I'm Jonas Redman. Call me Jonas."

Dimples bracketed her mouth as her smile deepened. "Thank you, Jonas. I'd be very grateful if you'd stay in the ranch house while my family is away."

"No, problem, ma'am. No trouble at all."

Yeah. Right. Who was he trying to kid? The woman was going to be trouble and then some.

Chapter Two

"Is Mr. Redman going to be taking his meals here?"

Alexa, who was sitting at an L-shaped bar at one end of the kitchen cabinets, looked up at the cook. Reena's question had caught her off guard. Jonas's meals were not something that had yet crossed her mind. Since she'd left the man's office a few minutes ago, the most she'd tried to do was convince herself that their paths would rarely cross.

"I don't know, Reena. I suppose I'll have to ask him. But don't worry about it. If he does decide to take his meals here instead of in the bunkhouse, then he'll just have to eat what Sassy and I eat."

Reena nodded. "I'll make plenty to go around."

The cook's remark only reminded Alexa all over again that she was going to have to deal with Jonas Redman being in the house. True, Sassy stayed in a room off the kitchen, but she slipped in and out at all hours of the night. Sassy was young, and so her free time was, more often than not, taken up with social activities. And evenings were exactly when Jonas would be showing up at the ranch house.

Alexa wasn't sure if she was excited or annoyed by the prospect. Something about the man left her uneasy. Just a few words from him had made her stop and take a second look at herself, and that in itself was scary. A wandering cowboy from Texas shouldn't have that much power over her. In fact, he shouldn't be having any effect on her at all.

With that thought, Alexa quickly rose from the bar stool. "I'd better check to see if Sassy has one of the guest rooms ready," she told Reena, then quickly exited the kitchen.

Upstairs, she met the young red-haired

maid in the hallway. A ball of sheets was wadded in her arms.

"Need something, Alexa?"

Alexa smiled. "I was just wondering if you've finished preparing a room for Jonas?"

Nodding, Sassy dropped the sheets and motioned for Alexa to follow her. "I've tidied up the room next to yours," she said as they walked toward the end of the hallway. "I hope that's okay. Since you didn't say, I thought you'd probably be wanting him near." She looked at Alexa. "I mean, in your condition you might need help in the middle of the night. If your water broke or something, you wouldn't want to have to go traipsing across the house to find him."

Everything Sassy was saying made sense. Yet the idea of Jonas in such close proximity was definitely going to be a challenge to Alexa's senses.

"I suppose you're right," Alexa reluctantly agreed.

The two women stepped into the room, and while Sassy gave another smoothing hand to the bedclothes, Alexa glanced around her. The room wasn't as large as hers, but with its rustic cedar furnishings, Native American artwork and woven rugs, it was fitting for a man like Jonas. As for Barry, he wouldn't have fit in anywhere on the Chaparral. He'd been a city boy through and through. Tailored suits, briefcases and wing-tipped oxfords were his everyday staples. Sometimes she wondered if she'd gotten involved with the man just because he had been so opposite from her home life, so opposite from Mitch.

For a moment, memories of the young cowboy assaulted her, freezing her footsteps and the images in her mind. Mitch had been her first love, and his reckless, carefree attitude toward life had been infectious to a teenage Alexa. She'd thought the world was theirs until one night, after too much beer and partying, he'd wrecked the truck they'd been riding in on a mountain highway east of Ruidoso. The crash had killed Mitch instantly and put Alexa in the hospital for over two weeks. The incident had drastically changed her life, and ever since she'd shied away from anything wearing boots and a sexy grin. Instead of the outdoor girl she'd always been, she'd turned bookish and serious and set her mind on a degree in political science. By age twenty she'd gotten a position on the mayor's staff in Ruidoso, and two years later she'd gone to work in the state capital building.

And there she'd believed she'd put cowboys and the Chaparral out of her mind.

Now here she was back home, doing something she'd never planned to do again. Thinking about a cowboy.

"Alexa—is something wrong?"

Alexa was so absorbed in her thoughts that it took Sassy's voice a moment or two to finally register with her. When it did, she looked across the room at the maid. "Did you say something?" she asked blankly.

"Is something wrong?" Sassy repeated. "You looked sorta sad."

Alexa did her best to smile. "Nothing is wrong. I was just thinking about something that happened a long time ago."

The maid didn't look too convinced but, thankfully, changed the subject.

"Oh. Well, I was asking if I should open the balcony door," she said. "Some fresh air might make the room smell nice."

"Go ahead," Alexa told her. "Jonas can close it later."

"And what about flowers? I wasn't sure about putting fresh flowers in the room."

Alexa walked over to the nightstand and wiped a finger over the polished wood. Everything was spotless. "No. I don't think

Jonas will expect flowers. He's probably not used to such things."

Sassy didn't respond, and Alexa glanced up to see a disapproving look on her face.

"Just because he's a cowboy doesn't mean he can't appreciate flowers," Sassy muttered after a moment.

Alexa opened her mouth to assure the young woman she didn't mean anything insulting with her remark. Everyone was treated equally at the Chaparral. But Sassy would hardly believe that now. Dear God, it seemed like everything she said today came out sounding wrong.

"I'd better go get the sheets in the wash," Sassy said and quickly started toward the door.

Alexa called out to her. "Wait a minute, Sassy. Please."

Alexa's heart softened as she watched the young woman walk back to the center of the room. Sassy had been orphaned at age seventeen, when her parents had perished in a house fire. After that, Alexa's parents had taken her in and given her a job here on the Chaparral. She'd become like family, and Alexa wanted her to understand that.

"You need something else, Alexa?" Sassy asked.

With a regretful smile, Alexa walked over and hugged the younger woman's shoulders. "Yes, I need to apologize. For sounding like a—well, like a queen wasp."

Sassy laughed. "Oh, Alexa, that's a terrible thing to say about yourself. I understand you've been under a strain. Moving back home like this...it's gotta be—well, something you'll have to get used to all over again."

Alexa sighed with relief. At least Sassy understood. "Truthfully, Sassy, it's turning out to be much harder than I ever expected. But I'll survive. I just wanted to say that bit about Jonas and the flowers—I honestly didn't want you putting flowers in his room, because I didn't want him to think I was going out of my way to make things extra pleasant for him."

Sassy's brows pulled together in confusion. "Why? He has to be a nice man or Quint wouldn't have hired him."

The young woman's simple reasoning made Alexa feel even smaller. "I'm sure he is. It's just that—well, it's kind of awkward for me—having him here in the house. I've only just met him and he's—"

"Darn good-looking," Sassy finished for her. "And single."

Alexa's brows lifted. "How did you know that about him?"

Sassy's smile was conspiring. "The ranch has a gossip grapevine, Alexa. I hear things from the bunkhouse cook."

"Gus? He's getting too old to gossip!"

"Don't let him hear you say that," Sassy joked, then looked at Alexa with empathy. "And don't go worrying about the new manager. Your mother will be back soon and everything will get back to normal."

Long after dark, Alexa was lounging on the back patio, soaking up the cool breeze and thinking about Sassy's comment. Would things in her life ever get back to normal? she wondered.

In spite of her blowup with Barry, she was excited about the coming baby. Already she loved it with all her heart. In fact, for the past few months, thoughts of her coming child were the only thing that had kept her focused and going. Yet she wondered if she'd ever

have the courage to trust another man or, for
that matter, to resume her job in Santa Fe.

When she'd left, she'd done so on a leave
of absence, with the option to return to Senator Hutchins's office whenever she was ready.
Which had been an overly generous offer on
the senator's part. Alexa appreciated the fact
that her job would be there for her if she decided to return. But she wasn't sure that life
in politics was right for her anymore. Barry
would still be hanging around the capital, and
though he'd been out of her life for months
now, she'd not been able to avoid running into
him casually.

The whole situation was awkward. But
then, she should have never been attracted
to Barry in the first place, she thought with
self-disgust. She should have been able to see
beneath his polished appearance and glib way
with words. Once she'd started dating him,
her instincts should have picked up on the fact
that he was out for himself and no one else.
Damn it, he'd been a lobbyist. What more
could she expect?

But he'd helped get great environmental
laws passed for the state and the good of the
people. She'd believed he was a sincere, dedi-

cated man. And she'd been drawn to him because of their shared interests and goals.

With Barry she'd approached their relationship with logic and common sense rather than passion, and she'd felt proud of herself for not swooning and falling into a pit of sexual heat, as she had with Mitch. They had dated and then moved in with each other about a year later. She'd thought they'd shared goals and ideals.

Eventually, when she'd learned she was pregnant, she'd been happy, envisioning the three of them as a perfect family. But only a few days later she'd learned quite by accident—through a stack of paperwork he'd left lying about in their apartment—that he'd been involved in some unscrupulous dealings. And to make matters worse, when she'd confronted him, he'd clearly felt no shame over his behavior.

When she'd announced to Barry that she was leaving, he'd been shocked that she would turn down such a catch as him. He'd considered himself a rising star in the state political arena, and he'd expected Alexa to want to ride on his coattails all the way to the top. But once she'd discovered his underhanded dealings, she'd had no choice but to end everything between them.

She couldn't live with an immoral man, much less have her child raised by one. Barry hadn't seen it that way, and for a few weeks he'd made ugly noises about custody rights and using his political pull to take the child completely away from her. That had been his way of forcing her into coming back to him.

But she and Barry had both known that he'd not really wanted her or the child that much. He simply hadn't wanted to lose the fight.

Fortunately, he'd eventually come to the conclusion that their relationship could never be salvaged. He'd decided that signing his rights to the baby over to her would be much better than Alexa's exposing his misdeeds to a pack of hungry newspaper reporters.

It was a relief to know that she was free of Barry now, she thought. She only wished she was free of the damage his betrayal had done to her self-confidence, her ability to judge people on the inside, where it really mattered.

A footfall on the concrete patio pulled Alexa from her glum thoughts, and she turned her head to see Jonas Redman standing a few feet away. A duffel bag was thrown over his shoulder, and he appeared tired and dusty. Foolish excitement hummed along her veins.

"Excuse me for interrupting, Alexa. I only wanted to let you know that I'm finally here. I meant to arrive earlier, but things got busy."

Her heart thumping, Alexa swung her legs to the ground and rose to her feet. "That's all right. If you'd like to come in, I'll show you your room."

Nodding, he followed her through the back door of a small atrium filled with all types of potted plants and cushioned lawn furniture, then into a dimly lit kitchen.

"Sassy is out for the evening," she informed him. "But Reena, our cook, saved supper for you."

"No need for that," Jonas replied. "I can eat with the boys in the bunkhouse. Gus will have something left over."

She gestured toward an open door that led into a long hallway. "It's no trouble, Jonas. And someone needs to help Sassy and me eat all the food that Reena prepares."

At the end of the hallway they turned into what looked to be a living room. On the left side, a wide staircase made of dark, polished wood led to the second floor. Jonas followed at a respectable distance. Until they were nearly to the landing. There, Alexa suddenly sagged against the bannister and clutched it tightly with both hands as though it was all she could do to stay upright.

Leaping up the two steps separating them, Jonas quickly put his hand under her elbow to steady her. As his eyes anxiously scanned her face, he noticed her breathing was labored.

"Alexa! What's wrong?"

Pressing a hand to her throat, she drew in a long breath. "I—I'm okay, Jonas. I just... got a little winded. That happens when I try to move too fast. All this extra weight pushing against my diaphragm doesn't make stair-climbing easy."

She was recovering quickly, yet he was reluctant to loosen his hold on her arm. If she happened to get dizzy and fall backward down the staircase, it would, in all likelihood, harm her and the baby.

"You didn't need to escort me to my room," he scolded lightly. "You could have just told me where it was."

Straightening to her full height, she said, "Don't be silly. I have to climb the stairs to get to my room, too."

As Jonas stared at her, he was suddenly struck by how soft her skin felt against his hand, how sweet she smelled and how totally vulnerable she was. It had been a long time since he'd been this close to a woman, a long time since he'd touched one. He'd almost forgotten the tender feelings a woman could evoke in a man.

"Are you having health problems?" he asked. "Something I need to know about?"

Color darkened her cheeks as she shook her head. "No. I'm fine. Really, Jonas."

Pulling her arm away from his hand, she headed up the stairs, leaving him with nothing to do but follow.

At the end of a wide hallway, she gestured to the right, where a door stood ajar. "This is your room. If there's anything you need that Sassy might have missed, just let me know."

Jonas entered the room and was surprised when she followed and switched on a lamp at the head of the bed. Earlier today, he'd gotten the impression that she wanted to avoid being near him at all cost. Maybe she was deciding he wasn't a threat, after all.

"The bathroom is over there in the right corner," she informed him. "And the balcony is beyond the open door. You might find it more comfortable to sleep with that door open. The night air cools the room nicely."

He tossed his duffel bag onto the bed. Everything he'd brought from Texas was in that bag. Including his weapon and Ranger badge. He was going to have to find a hiding place for them. Otherwise, the maid might possibly stumble across the items during her routine cleaning.

"Everything is fine, Alexa. The room is far beyond my needs." He lifted off his hat and placed it next to the bag. "I'll be out of here early in the morning, so I'll try not to disturb you. As for the evenings, I can't say when I'll be showing up. I'm sure you remember that ranch days rarely end before dark."

Nodding, she gave him a brief smile. "Of course. When my father was running the ranch, he was oftentimes a stranger around here. So I don't expect your schedule to fit with mine. You're welcome to come and go as you please."

Strange how she'd done an about-face, Jonas thought. She'd initially been outraged when he'd suggested staying in the house with her. Now she was the perfect welcoming hostess. Was that what being pregnant did to a woman, swung her moods wildly one direction and then another? If so, he was going to be in for a hell of a ride in these next coming days.

She started toward the door. "If you'll come down to the kitchen in a few minutes, I'll heat your supper."

Jonas was hardly expecting her, the heiress of the place, to see to his kitchen needs, but he wasn't going to argue the point now. If she wanted to extend to him a bit of hospitality, then he was going to be grateful enough to accept it.

"Fine. Thanks."

She disappeared into the hallway, and he began to put away his things in the long oak dresser. As for his pistol and badge, he pulled out the bottom drawer of the dresser, placed them on the floor beneath, then returned the drawer to its track and shoved it back in place.

Minutes later, after a quick shower, Jonas pulled on a pair of faded jeans and boots and topped them with a white T-shirt before heading downstairs. As he walked toward the kitchen, he was struck by the quietness and reminded all over again that no one was in the house except for him and Alexa.

The smell of roast beef and vegetables met his nose long before he entered the kitchen.

The growl of his stomach reminded him that he'd not eaten a bite of food since breakfast.

"I didn't know whether you would prefer iced tea or beer with your meal," Alexa told him as he stepped into the room. "So I gave you both."

A plate piled high with food was already laid out on the table. Next to it was a basket full of bread rolls, an assortment of condiments and the two drinks. She gestured for him to take a seat.

"Aren't you going to have any?" he asked as he pulled out a chair.

"I would, but I've already eaten," she told him.

"Then surely you can join me with something to drink," he suggested politely.

She studied him for a long moment, as though she couldn't quite decide whether joining him would be the right thing to do. Jonas tried not to let her attitude offend him. After all, she'd already gone out of her way to be gracious. No one said she had to cozy up to him.

"All right. Since it's decaffeinated, I suppose I could have a glass of tea," she told him as she went over to the counter to fetch the drink.

"You're not supposed to have caffeine?" he asked curiously.

"It's not healthy for the baby, so I try to limit the stuff."

She carried the tea back over to the table and took the chair across from him. He glanced up from his plate to see her stirring a spoonful of sugar into her glass. There was a small ruby and silver ring on her right hand, but nothing on her left. The lack of an engagement ring spoke volumes to Jonas.

"Sorry if my questions sound silly. I don't know much about women having babies. Cows and horses are more my line."

Tonight, without a hat and a button-down shirt, he looked different somehow, Alexa thought. Younger and sexier, if that was possible. His brown hair was the color of a pecan streaked with shades of coffee and honey. The waves stuck out in damp disarray about his head, as though he'd had an expensive razor cut to make his hair look purposely messy. But Alexa very much doubted he spent his money on such vain things. It didn't fit his nature, she decided, as her gaze dipped down to his corded arms. They had a farmer's tan that ended at the cuffs of his T-shirt, and

Alexa found herself wondering what his chest looked like beneath the white T-shirt.

Swallowing at the nervous tightening in her throat, she asked, "You don't have any children of your own?"

He shook his head. "No. I'm divorced. Have been for six years."

The revelation jarred her. For some reason, she'd pictured him as always being a single man. To think that he'd once loved and married a woman put him in a whole new light.

"Oh. I'm sorry. I didn't mean to pry."

One thick shoulder shrugged. "You weren't. And it's not a secret."

What had happened? Alexa wondered. Had he been at fault for the breakup of his marriage? Or his wife? Was his ex the reason he'd left Texas?

Forget it, Alexa. This man's personal life is not your business. Besides, you have your own problems to think about.

After a short stretch of silence, he said, "So you've been living in Santa Fe. Did you like living in the city?"

Alexa slid her fingertips up and down the side of the ice-cold glass. "It was okay." At least it was okay until everything with Barry had gone wrong, she thought grimly.

"I worked at the state capital building as an aide to a senator."

Feeling his gaze on her, she darted a glance at him and was surprised to see that he actually looked curious. Most men, especially the outdoor type, never showed much interest in her job. Maybe her first impression of Jonas Redman had been right. He wasn't an ordinary man.

"You like that sort of thing—working in government?"From out of nowhere a bit of shyness struck her, and she looked down at the tabletop rather than at him. "It's interesting to me. But mostly I like helping serve the public."

"How did you get the job with the senator? I suspect there were plenty of applicants waiting in line."

Lifting her gaze back to him, she was relieved to see he was now focusing on his plate rather than her face. "I honestly don't know how I happened to land it. At the time I was working in the Ruidoso mayor's office and trying to finish up college." She chuckled with fond remembrance. "What I lacked in experience, I made up in enthusiasm, I suppose."

He looked at her and smiled, and for a moment Alexa felt as though everything around her stopped. The expression warmed his face and hinted at a softer side to the iron cowboy. It also endeared him to her, pulled her toward him in a way that caught her by complete surprise.

"Are you planning to go back? I mean, after your baby is born?"

A soft sigh escaped her as she turned her gaze away from him and toward the row of windows to their right. Even though it was dark, a distant outdoor lamp illuminated a part of the ranch yard. At the moment, nothing was stirring except for the wind ruffling the leaves on the aspen trees. "I—I'm not sure. I think I need a little time to make up my mind about that."

"I'm curious about one thing," he said.

His comment jerked her gaze back to his. "What's that?"

He reached for another roll and proceeded to tear it down the center. "I've been wondering about your feelings for this ranch. It appears your father and brother put their lives into making it go. Were you never interested in it?"

Interested? Once she'd loved every inch, every blade of grass, every cow and horse on the place. Even before she'd started kindergarten, she'd followed her father around, watching him tend to everything, from a sick calf to a broken fence. He'd put her in the saddle before she'd been able to walk, and from her early childhood up until Mitch's death she'd had one purpose in life, and that had been to help run the ranch, to do her part in making it grow and prosper. The accident had turned her away from everything she'd once loved, and now, after all this time, she was frightened to let herself love it again.

"Of course I was," she said stiffly. "The ranch has always been my home."

His plate nearly empty, he put down his fork and leaned back in his chair. Alexa hated the way her eyes were drawn to the broad width of his chest, the bunching of his biceps as he folded his arms together.

"Well," he said casually, "most women don't get involved with the grit and grime of everyday ranch life. Quint says your mother doesn't ride at all. Do you?"

His question seemed so absurd to Alexa that she couldn't stop herself from laughing. Which only prompted him to look at her in a calculating way.

"I didn't realize that was a funny question," he said as her laughter ebbed to a soft chuckle.

"I'm sorry. I couldn't help it." She leaned toward him and smiled, with the first confidence she'd felt in a long, long time. "If I wasn't so pregnant, I bet I could outride you, Jonas Redman."

His hazel eyes suddenly glinted with interest; at the same time, a grin tugged at one corner of his mouth. "That's a bold statement. Especially since you don't know me."

"Maybe. But I know myself. I've been riding since before I could walk. In spite of Mother's protest."

"She didn't want you to do those types of things?"

Alexa grimaced. "Mother was always a worrier. She did her best to keep Quint and me from doing anything she considered risky. But Dad won out on the riding and…other things."

"In other words it was the risk she opposed. It wasn't that she wanted her daughter to do more feminine things."

"That's right. You see, Mother had—well, she had two sons by her first husband that she…had to give up for a long time. And I guess she protected me and my brother because she was afraid she'd lose us, too."

Now why had she gone and told him all that? Alexa wondered. It wasn't like her to share family matters with strangers. Especially such things as her mother had gone through.

Because Jonas doesn't feel like a stranger. Because something about him is easy and calm and inviting.

"That's only human," he said softly. "We want to cling to what we love the most."

A long rush of air passed her lips, and she realized her heart was thumping hard behind her breasts. When she'd heated Jonas's supper for him, she'd not expected to join him, much less have such a personal conversation with the man. She'd planned to go about her business or pretend to have more important things to do and politely leave the kitchen.

He hadn't allowed that to happen, and now all she could think about was that the two of them were alone, that only a wall would be separating them as they slept.

Dear God, what was the matter with her? Were her hormones going crazy all of a sudden? Since her break with Barry, the idea of even looking at another man had repulsed her.

And Jonas Redman wasn't her type at all. No, cowboys were off-limits. Forever.

And now politicians are off-limits, too. What are you going to do, Alexa? Quit men entirely because you happen to be a bad judge of character? You've tried passion, and you've tried logic. Is there anything left?

Clearing her throat, she slowly rose to her feet. "Uh—it's getting late. Is there anything else you'd like before I head upstairs?"

Pushing his chair away from the table, he also stood. "I've had plenty. Thanks."

He picked up his dirty plate, glass and beer bottle. "Where do I put these?" he asked.

She motioned to the sink. "Just put them there. Sassy will put them in the dishwasher later."

Alexa left the kitchen, but he quickly caught up to her in the living room, just before she reached the staircase. When his hand came under her elbow and his arm circled around the back of her waist, she stopped in her tracks and stared at him.

"May I ask what you're doing?"

His solemn expression didn't waver. "You're not going up those stairs without me to help you."

Her first instinct was to laugh, but she bit

back the urge. As she looked at his face, she realized he was seriously concerned for her, and suddenly the idea that he cared that much for her well-being caused tears to sting the back of her eyes.

"I have to go up and down them during the day, Jonas," she said softly.

"Yes. But it's late and you're tired. I'm here now. So don't argue."

A smile tugged at her lips. "All right. It would be nice to lean on your strong arm."

"That's better," he said huskily, then urged her forward.

He purposely kept their climb at a slow pace, and although Alexa realized he was taking it easy for her sake, she was quickly wishing the task would end. Having Jonas's arm locked firmly around her, feeling the warmth of his hard body pressing against the side of hers, was doing strange things to her senses.

Once they reached the landing, she expected him to release her, but his arm remained at her back and his fingers stayed curled around her arm until they reached Alexa's bedroom door.

"Here we are," he said, "and you're not even breathing hard."

No. But her heart was hammering, and

every nerve in her body sizzling, she thought. "Thank you, Jonas. Good night."

Dropping his hold on her, he started to his room, only to pause and look over his shoulder at her. "You know, after your baby gets here, I might just put you to that riding test."

She pushed a smile on her face. "I'll be ready."

Who was she kidding? Alexa thought bitterly as she entered the bedroom and shut the door firmly behind her. She'd not been on a horse in years. She'd not even touched a bridle or saddle or even pulled on a pair of boots since she moved away from the Chaparral.

What in heck had she been doing, telling Jonas all that stuff, acting as though she remembered how to be a cowgirl? Why had she told him such things in the first place? Why had she wanted him to know that part of her life? In Santa Fe, she'd kept that part of her past all carefully tucked away, while she tried to be a smooth, polished lady, rubbing elbows with powerful people in powerful places.

Dear God, she'd believed she'd matured into an intelligent woman, one wise enough to make good, practical choices for herself. But all that careful planning and the cautious approach she'd taken with Barry had been for naught. Now she was afraid to trust any man. And even more afraid to trust herself.

Chapter Three

Nearly a week later she was sitting in a small office off the downstairs den, writing the last payroll check, when a knock sounded at the open door.

Expecting it to be Sassy, wielding a dusting cloth, she was more than surprised to see Jonas. The past few days she'd spoken to him only twice, as he'd helped her up the stairs at night. Those conversations had been brief and polite, ending far before Alexa had wanted them to. And one evening, as she'd sat out on her balcony, she'd happened to spot him walking across the ranch yard.

"Hello, Jonas," she said now, her heart

skipping to a hard, fast beat. "Won't you come in?"

He politely removed his hat as he stepped into the room, and as Alexa looked at him, she couldn't help but notice a hint of fatigue on his face. Apparently he considered it his obligation as the ranch's general manager to work day and night.

"I don't want to interrupt," he said as he crushed the brim of his hat between his fists. "I'm heading into town to the feed store and I wondered if you'd like to ride in with me. Since Reena told me that you've not been off the place, I thought you might need a change of scenery."

She was more than shocked by his invitation. Especially since he'd not so much as exchanged a word with her since their night in the kitchen.

Alexa glanced down at her red jersey top and blue jeans. "I'm not exactly dressed for going to town. But I suppose it doesn't matter." She began to gather the papers scattered in front of her. "Can you give me five minutes to put all this stuff away and tidy up?"

"Sure. I'll be waiting on the front porch," he told her.

He disappeared out the door, and Alexa

hurriedly locked all her paperwork in a file cabinet. Once that was done, she fetched her purse, swiped on a dab of lipstick and headed to the porch.

When she stepped outside Jonas was speaking into his cell phone, but when he spotted her, he abruptly ended the call and slipped the instrument in his pocket. Alexa didn't catch any of his words, but from the sheepish expression on his face, she wondered if he'd been speaking to another woman.

"If the call was important I'll go back in and wait," she told him.

"I'll deal with the call later," he said briskly, then gave her a half smile. "I'm glad you decided to go with me."

"I am, too," she said and realized it was true.

He'd pulled one of the ranch's trucks to the front of the drive so that Alexa had only a short distance to walk. After he helped her into the cab, he settled himself behind the wheel and turned the vehicle down the long lane lined with tall ponderosa pines.

"I normally send one of the hands in to town to fetch things we need," he said as they reached a graveled country road. "But Quint wants me to take a look at some new horse feed made from coconuts. It's high-powered protein, and supposedly it takes half as much to feed one horse. I'm skeptical, but if he thinks it's worth looking into, I'll keep an open mind."

"Grandfather must have put Quint on to the idea of the coconut feed," Alexa said. "He's always looking at new things in the industry."

"From the way Quint talks, your grandfather is quite a character. Just how old is he, anyway?"

"Abe is eighty-four. But he thinks he's forty-four."

"Hmm. Well, I admire him without ever having met him. Any man that can keep an open mind about progress at that age has to be a good man."

Beneath lowered lashes, Alexa allowed her gaze to sweep over the long length of him. His jeans were faded and worn, but his brown boots were expensive ostrich, and his green-and-white-striped shirt had a tailored look to it. Since she'd just written out the payroll, she knew exactly what the ranch was paying him for his services. It was a handsome amount, but not the sort that would support wearing a couple-hundred-dollar pair of boots in a cow pasture. The idea made her wonder if he'd come from a moneyed family. Yet if that were the case, he'd probably be working his own ranch instead of someone else's, she decided.

"If you'd like, we'll drive over to Apache Wells, my grandfather's ranch, some time soon, and I'll introduce you," she said after a moment. "Gramps always likes company, and I've not seen him in a while."

He glanced at her and she could see her invitation had surprised him. Frankly, she'd surprised herself. This past week, she'd done her best to keep the man pushed out of her thoughts. Yet each night when she'd climbed the stairs to her bedroom, she'd missed him at her side. Missed the warmth of his hands, the tender concern on his face. And later, in bed, she'd wondered what kind of lover he might be.

"That's sounds nice," he said.

For some reason the baby must have known her thoughts needed to be hauled back to order. He or she was doing flips and kicks, and Alexa unconsciously splayed her hand over the movement in her stomach.

"You've been very busy this week," she commented. "I've not seen you coming and going in the house."

He darted another glance at her, then

frowned as he noticed her hand pressing against her abdomen. "What's wrong? Are you hurting?"

"No. Everything is fine. The little guy is just doing a tumbling act, that's all."

His features relaxed. "Oh. So you know it's a boy?"

Alexa shook her head. "No. I'm old-fashioned. I want to learn the sex of the baby the natural way."

"Is that what you want? A boy?"

Shrugging, she looked out the window. Whenever he talked to her about the baby, it made her sad. His interest seemed genuine, and she could only wonder why Barry couldn't have been an honorable man, a father her child could have admired and looked up to. Instead, he'd been bent on acquiring power and money in ways that would no doubt eventually land him in deep trouble.

God, she'd not really known the man at all. And yet all she had to do was look at Jonas and she instinctively knew he was a man who would never take his responsibilities lightly, that he would put others before himself. Or was she seeing only what she wanted to see? she thought doubtfully. How could she know such things about Jonas Redman? Was she fooling herself again? Still, she couldn't deny a bond was forming between them.

"I just want a healthy child," she answered. "That's all that matters."

"I suppose your doctor is in Santa Fe. Do you plan to go up there to deliver?"

Alexa shook her head. "No. My doctor referred me to a good physician in Ruidoso. I wanted to be close to home when the baby is born."

Jonas nodded that he understood and then focused his attention on the two-lane highway winding through the pine-covered mountains. After several minutes passed in silence, Alexa was convinced his thoughts had moved on to other things, until suddenly he spoke again.

"Alexa, I know this is none of my business, but I can't help thinking about the baby's father. Is he going to be around? I mean, when the baby is born?"

A grimace tightened her features. "No. He's been out of my life for—well, for several months now. He... It turned out he wasn't ready for a wife and child. And it was easy to decide that I needed to move on."

"That's too bad."

He sounded as though he truly was sorry that things hadn't worked out for her, and Alexa was touched by his sincerity. Maybe since he'd gone through a divorce of his own, he understood how humiliating and crushing it was to discover that love wasn't what you'd dreamed and hoped it would be.

But she hadn't really loved Barry. She'd pretended. She'd tried to convince herself that he made her heart beat fast, that he was the man she wanted to grow old with, share her dreams with. She'd believed living with a man that held a similar job to hers would make everything just perfect and happy. She'd been utterly wrong about that, about him, and so many other things.

"Please don't feel sorry for me, Jonas. I'm much better off without Barry in my life. He wasn't good for me."

"If that's the case, then why did you—"

"Get involved with him?" Alexa finished for him. "That's a good question. I thought he was a good man. But he turned out to be totally different than I'd first believed. Has that ever happened to you?"

His expression grim, he stared straight ahead. "More times than you can imagine."

* * *

Ten minutes later they entered Ruidoso and, figuring Alexa had no interest in joining him at the feed store, Jonas offered to drop her off wherever she'd like.

He left her at a small dress boutique on Main Street, then drove to Rogers Grain and Tack on the east end of town. As he maneuvered the truck through the traffic, he wondered what was wrong with him. He shouldn't have asked Alexa about her ex-beau or whatever the hell the man had been to her. The guy was none of his business. Neither he nor Alexa had anything to do with Jonas's reason for being in New Mexico. So why wasn't he thinking about his job instead of about a pregnant ranching heiress?

Because something about her reminded him of all the dreams and plans he'd once had for himself and Celia. Like the children they would have and making a little ranch into a fine place to raise them. Jonas had the little ranch now. But not the children or the wife. And he had no one to blame for that but himself, he thought grimly.

Five minutes later, Jonas parked the truck in front of the feed store. As he stepped inside the store, a cowbell clanged above the door. To his immediate left, a middle-aged man with graying hair stood behind a long glass counter. Along the back wall, two cowboys were rifling through rows of hanging bits and spurs.

"Afternoon," the man behind the counter greeted. "Can I help you with something?"

Nodding, Jonas explained why he was there, and the clerk motioned for him to step behind the counter and follow down a narrow hallway to the right.

"The feed is in the back, in the grain room. You're welcome to look all you want," the clerk said as they passed through a wide wooden door. "Sales on the stuff are beginning to pick up. 'Course, it always takes something new a while to catch hold. You know how some people are—want to stick to tradition."

The grain room, as the clerk called it, was a huge, barnlike area with high ceilings and a wooden planked floor. Tons and tons of sacked grain, feed and seed were stacked to the rafters. Across the way, a pickup truck was backed up to a loading dock. A tall man with black hair and a handlebar mustache was standing to one side, while a worker loaded the truck with sacks of cooked oats, which were most commonly fed to racehorses.

"Well, I manage the Chaparral for the Cantrell family," Jonas explained to the clerk. "Quint's considering changing the feeding program for the horses."

The clerk stopped in front of a particular pile of sacks and opened one that was already sitting on the floor. Reaching into the heavy paper sack, Jonas pulled out a handful of pellets and lifted them to his nose. They smelled fruity, and he figured the sweetness would please the horses.

"Oh," the clerk said in a friendly way, "you must be the new man Quint told me about. You come from Texas, he said."

"That's right." Jonas gestured toward the feed. "How much would a ton of this stuff cost?"

"Don't know. These days the cost fluctuates almost every day—what with the cost of fuel and all. I'd have to figure it up for you. But you have to remember, it only takes half as much as regular feed. Cuts your cost in two."

"You say you're from Texas, mister?"

The blunt question came from behind Jonas, and he turned to see the man with the mustache standing a few steps behind him. There was a clench to his jaw and a flinty look in his eye that said he was just itching for a fight. Which didn't make any sense. Jonas had never seen the man before in his life.

"I did. San Antonio." He wanted to ask the man if he had any problem with that, but having a saloon fight in a feed store wasn't a part of his duties as a Texas Ranger. Not unless it was absolutely necessary.

"You managing the Chaparral now?" the man asked curtly.

"Right again," Jonas said coolly.

The man's jaw grew even tighter. "Good! Because I want to know what in hell your men thought they were doing when they cut the fence to my back pasture!"

Leaving the stunned clerk behind, Jonas closed the space between him and the angry cowboy. "Maybe you'd better explain. I've not heard about any cut fence."

"Three weeks ago I found a herd of mama cows belonging to the Chaparral on my property. The fence was cut in two different places, then patched back with wire that wouldn't hold. Me and my hands spent a whole day repairing it and another day running your cattle back where they belonged."

The cogs in Jonas's head were suddenly turning. "Sorry. I didn't catch your name, mister."

"This is Tyler Pickens," the clerk interjected as he introduced both men.

Diplomacy and a need to gather all the information he could forced Jonas to say, "Well, Mr. Pickens, I apologize if any of my men caused the problem. I would have thought you'd have let Quint or me know about this problem before now."

"Everybody knows Quint isn't at the Chaparral anymore," Tyler retorted. "I tried contacting him over at Abe's place but could never catch up to him. The old man told me that I needed to talk to you."

Damn it. This could have been the break Jonas needed, and he was learning about it three weeks after the fact.

"Why haven't you talked to me before now?" asked Jonas.

"I was away from the ranch for a couple of weeks. I've had other things to do—or so you ought to know," Tyler snarled.

Jonas did his best to remain cool. Finding rustlers was a far bigger priority to him than giving this man an attitude adjustment.

"Well, now that we're talking, I can assure

you that the Chaparral will be more than glad to cover any fencing costs and labor spent on your part. I take it your property runs adjacent to the Chaparral?"

"Two miles of it."

"Can you show me the spots where the fence was downed?"

"Damned right!" Tyler cursed. "It's not far off the road. Maybe a hundred yards or more. I can't understand it. Quint's hands have never been a rowdy bunch before."

"What makes you think they cut the fence?" Jonas countered.

The agitated rancher threw up his hands. "Who else? That area is several miles off the beaten track. Wouldn't be any reason for anyone else to be back in the mountains."

"What about your own hands?" Jonas quizzed. "Would they have any reason to cut the fence?"

"Hell, no! They don't like building fence any better than I do!"

Reaching into his jeans pocket, Jonas pulled out his wallet and fished out a card. Handing it to the rancher, he said, "My name is Jonas Redman. My telephone number is there. I'd appreciate it if you'd give me a call whenever you have time to show me the area where the fence was down. In the meantime, I'll talk to Quint about this and come up with compensation for your time and material."

Suddenly Tyler's expression relaxed, and he shook his head. Apparently now that he had vented his steam, he wanted to forget the whole matter. "No need for that. Quint and his family have always been good neighbors. I guess it wasn't his fault that some of your hands decided to pull a prank."

Jonas was more than certain the incident wasn't a prank. But he could hardly relate such a thing to this man, who might in turn say something to his men. Before long everyone in the county would be talking about cattle rustlers, and the persons behind the crime would likely be alerted.

"Mr. Pickens, have you lost any cattle in the past few months?" asked Jonas.

"No. What does that have to do with anything?"

"Nothing," Jonas muttered. "Just give me a call whenever you have a chance. I'd be grateful."

Jonas was late getting back to the boutique. When he pulled the truck into a parking space

Alexa was already sitting on a bench in front of the little shop.

Before she had a chance to lift herself and the bags she was holding, he hurried over to assist her. "Sorry I'm late, Alexa. It took longer than I thought to order the feed."

She smiled at him. "No need to apologize. I'm enjoying the beautiful sunshine and being out among people."

He lifted the bags from her lap, then with a hand beneath her elbow, gently helped her to her feet. Today she smelled like a rose, and her hair was piled in curls atop her head. Loose tendrils tickled the back of her neck and touched the silver hoops dangling from her ears. She was the softest, sexiest woman he'd ever been around. Yet her condition constantly reminded him of her vulnerability and how much he wanted to protect her.

None of these feelings made sense to Jonas. Especially when he understood that he couldn't act on them. Yet he couldn't seem to stop the unbidden emotions. Not a good thing for a man who always liked to be in control of a situation.

"I see you've done some shopping," he commented.

She laughed softly. "Some things to wear

after the baby comes. Hopefully, I'll look like a woman again instead of a barrel." She looked at him. "What about the feed?"

"I purchased two ton. The store will be delivering it to the ranch this evening." He glanced at his watch, then on up the sidewalk. "Is there some place around here where we can have coffee or something before we head back?"

"There's the Blue Mesa up the street," she suggested.

"Can you walk the distance?" he asked.

She folded her arm through his. "Of course. It's only a block from here."

The day was sunny and very warm, and the sidewalk was full of people visiting the local shops, which constituted a large portion of the mountain tourist town. As they walked along, Jonas couldn't remember a time he'd strolled along a sidewalk in the afternoon with a woman on his arm. He and Celia had gone places together but had only hopped from the car into a restaurant or store, and that had always been at night. This walk with Alexa felt very different. Very family.

On the next block, they reached the Blue Mesa, a small restaurant constructed of pine logs. To the left of the building, outdoor tables and chairs were grouped on a wooden deck.

"Would you like to sit inside or out?" Alexa asked. "Either is fine with me."

"The day is beautiful. Let's stay out," he said.

She smiled as though she wholly approved of his choice. "Great."

With his hand at her back, they climbed three short stairs to the deck, then chose a spot in one corner, where shade dappled the table. A small stream tinkled several yards below them.

While they waited for their orders, Jonas brought up his encounter at Rogers Grain and Tack. "I met your neighbor at the feed store."

Her brows arched with curiosity. "Oh? Which one?"

"Tyler Pickens."

She grimaced. "Oh. Yes, his spread is north of ours. I think it connects to Chaparral land in a few spots."

"What do you know about him?"

A comical frown puckered her forehead. "You sound like a detective or something."

Jonas forced an easy smile to his face. It had been a long time since he'd gotten personal on an undercover assignment. He needed to remember not to let his questions sound practiced. "Sorry. It's just that Mr. Pickens and I didn't have what you'd call a warm meeting. He was hotter than a cur dog at roundup. Someone cut the fence—he thinks it was Chaparral hands."

Alexa was clearly insulted. "That's ridiculous. Our men would never destroy someone else's property, or ours. We don't hire those sorts!"

Frankly, Jonas didn't think so either. He'd been around the men for almost a month now, and all of them appeared to be responsible guys.

"I tried to smooth his feathers. And I'm going to have a look at the places where the fence was downed. Apparently some Chaparral cattle got onto his land, and he wasn't too happy about it. Has this sort of thing ever happened before?"

Alexa thought for a moment. "No. Not that I can remember. But then, while I lived in Santa Fe I heard only bits and pieces about the happenings on the ranch." She sighed, then shook her head. "But I wouldn't worry about Ty Pickens. Everyone knows he's a recluse of sorts. He doesn't like anyone even looking across his land, much less stepping foot on it. No wonder the man isn't married. He'd be hell and then some to live with."

To Jonas's amazement, he felt a prick of jealousy. Which made no sense at all. He didn't have any rights to Alexa. And he never would. "Sounds like you know the man personally."

Before Alexa could reply, a waitress arrived with their orders of cherry pie and coffee. Once she'd served them and moved away, Alexa answered, "Not at all. Down through the years we've tried to be friendly with him, and he showed up at a few functions that my parents hosted on the ranch. But he's one of those quiet sorts that no one really ever gets to know. You know what I mean?"

"Exactly."

For the next few moments they ate in silence. Yet in spite of the lack of conversation, Jonas found his gaze drawn back to her lovely face. For the past six years, since his divorce from Celia, he'd not felt much attraction toward any woman. In fact, he'd mostly put dating on the back burner and promised himself that someday, when his job didn't consume his life, he'd try being a husband again.

But being a Ranger was who he was, what he was. His marriage to Celia had ended because he'd not made enough time to share with her. He'd tried, but obviously it hadn't been enough to suit her. He couldn't yet find the courage to go through that hellish push and pull with another woman. No matter how much he wanted her.

"So do you have family back in Texas?" she asked as she lifted the coffee mug to her lips.

"Two siblings. An older sister, Bethany, and a younger brother, Bart," he said. "My father died nearly twenty years ago, and since then my mother has remarried and moved to California."

"Oh. And here I was feeling sorry for myself because I lost my father last year," she said sheepishly. "You must have lost your father at a very young age."

"I was fifteen. His death changed my life," he said honestly.

"What happened to him?"

Jonas knew he should keep his words measured, but he couldn't. Alexa was the first person he'd met in a long time that he wanted to talk to.

"He died of a sudden heart attack. You see, Curtis Redman was a police chief. He lived under an enormous amount of stress, and it got to him."

Sympathy was in her eyes as she scanned his face. "After going through something like that, it doesn't surprise me that you'd want to be a rancher rather than follow your dad into law."

Jonas stared at the remainder of his pie as a sense of guilt washed over him. He wasn't being totally dishonest with her. He really was a rancher. He owned several hundred acres just east of San Antonio, and he raised cattle and a few horses on the land. He just couldn't tell her that his father's death had done the very opposite of what she suspected. It hadn't turned him away from being in law enforcement; it had pushed him straight toward being a Ranger. His father had needed competent officers on his roster, but none of the moral, upstanding men of the community had wanted to take jobs in law enforcement and put their lives on the line. After he'd died, Jonas was determined to spend his life serving rather than taking.

"I like ranching," he murmured. "And the Chaparral is a nice place to work."

To his surprise she reached across the little table and touched her fingers to his. "I'm glad you think so."

He'd messed up, he thought. He should have never followed Reena's hint and invited Alexa to join him on this trip to town. But damn it, he'd been thinking of her all week and he'd been so busy he'd hardly had a chance to see her, much less speak to her. He'd told himself he needed to spend a bit of time with her this afternoon, just to make sure she was doing well. He'd not planned on their time together feeling so intimate, so good that he didn't want it to end.

Clearing his throat, he reached for his coffee and she pulled her hand back and rested it on her mound of a stomach. As he darted a glance at her, he realized that the baby growing inside her made her just that much more womanly to him.

"Have you been feeling well?" he asked.

She smiled. "I feel like I weigh a ton. But other than that, I'm fine. I see the doctor in three days. He'll let me know if something isn't right. But the baby is playing circus, so he or she must be happy."

"That's good. Quint would have my hide if anything happened to his sister."

Her blue eyes leveled on his face. "Is that the only reason for your concern?"

He'd not expected her to pose such a blunt question, and for a moment it took him aback. He could feel a flush of heat crawling up his neck as he said, "I'm not made of steel, Alexa. I want you and the baby to be safe, too."

"Thank you," she said softly.

A quirk of a smile touched his mouth, and then he turned his attention to eating the last of his pie. A few minutes later he suggested they go, and Alexa agreed. However, once they were off the restaurant deck, she asked if he'd like to walk down to the stream to see if they might spot some trout.

Not wanting to disappoint her, Jonas agreed, and with his hand firmly ensconced around her arm, they walked down a beaten dirt path until they reached the little stream shaded by pines and blue spruce.

"Oh! There goes a trout! See!" She pointed to the small fish darting among the boulders. "Do you fish, Jonas?"

"No. Never got into the sport."

Her arm was so soft and warm, and standing next to her so inexplicably sweet, that Jonas kept his hold on her, in spite of the fact that she no longer needed his support.

"I'm not surprised," she replied. "Cowboys are rarely fishermen. They think the sport is for geeks."

Jonas chuckled. "Oh, I don't know about that. We don't have to be macho men all the time."

She glanced up at him just as he gazed off at the tall mountain rising up in the near distance.

"That's Sierra Blanca Peak," she explained. "The Ski Apache resort is up there. Do you ski?"

"No. Never had the opportunity to learn. Do you?"

Her smile was tinged with a mixture of affection and sadness. "Yes. Mitch and I used to go skiing quite often. But that was before he died."

Startled by her words, Jonas glanced at her. "Who was Mitch? A relative?"

Shaking her head, she said, "No. He was a young cowboy who worked on the Chaparral. In fact, in many ways you remind me of him."

Interest peaked his brows. "Hmm. I hope that's a compliment."

Her gaze on the mountain, she allowed a wry smile to slant her lips. "I guess it is," she murmured. "You see, I was in love with him."

Chapter Four

For a moment Jonas was too stunned to say anything. Comparing him to a man she'd once loved was not anything he'd ever expected to hear from Alexa Cantrell.

"What happened to Mitch?" he finally managed to ask.

A soft sigh escaped her lips, and then she turned a smile on him that was both sad and sweet. "Forgive me, Jonas. The day is so beautiful, and it depresses me to talk about Mitch. I don't want to ruin our outing. But I'll tell you about it someday—when the time is right. Okay?"

"Sure."

With his hand on her arm he guided her away from the stream and back to the truck. As they walked, he felt as though the ground was tilting beneath his feet. She'd spoken of the man called Mitch with such affection and longing. Much more so than the father of her baby. Clearly the young cowboy had meant a great deal to her. What had she meant when she'd compared him to her lost love? Jonas wondered shakily. Was she trying to tell him that she was attracted to him, maybe even falling in love with him?

Hell, Jonas, that's about the stupidest thing that's ever crossed your mind. You only met the woman a week ago, and the time you've spent with her wouldn't fill up one whole day on the calendar. Besides, why would she want a man like you? She's a rich ranching heiress, and she thinks you're a nobody. Compared to her, you are *a nobody.*

"Is there any other place you'd like to stop by before we leave town?" he asked as he helped her into the cab of the truck.

"Thanks for asking, Jonas. But I have everything I need."

He paused at the open door and watched her buckle the seat belt and adjust the strap beneath the mound of baby.

"Then I guess we'll head home," he said.

Nodding, she smiled. "Yes. That's a nice sound, isn't it? Home. I hope you're beginning to think of the Chaparral as your home, Jonas."

"Of course I am. You're making it easy to do that, Alexa."

As her eyes connected with his, the smile fell from her face. For a split second Jonas forgot that they were parked along a busy street and that a few feet away people were strolling up and down the sidewalk. Something about the look on her face made him want to lean his head in to hers, made him want to kiss her plush lips.

The happy shriek of a nearby child suddenly broke his trance, and Jonas awkwardly cleared his throat as he shut the door, then walked around to the driver's side.

Their trip home seemed to pass more quickly. Maybe that was because Jonas was enjoying listening to her chatter about the ranch and a few of the horses she'd owned and ridden in her younger days.

By the time they reached the Chaparral, Jonas was beginning to see that she was far from the woman he'd first imagined her to be. She was warmer, sweeter, stronger. And he was far too charmed for his own good.

"Thank you for the outing, Jonas. It was very enjoyable," she told him once he'd parked in front of the ranch house and helped her to the ground.

"I enjoyed it, too," he admitted. He took her bags from the backseat of the truck. "I'll carry these in for you."

"There's no need. They weigh practically nothing."

"I'll carry them just the same," he told her.

They entered the house and Alexa was showing him where to put the bags when Sassy came bounding into the living room.

"Alexa? Where have you been? Frankie's been calling from Texas and she—" The young woman broke off in mid-sentence, a look of surprise on her face as she spotted Jonas standing a few feet away. "Oh— I'm sorry! I didn't know you had company. I mean—I thought you were alone."

"It's all right, Sassy. Jonas and I just got back from town," Alexa explained. "Has something happened with my mother?"

"No. She was all excited about something. Maybe you should call her," Sassy suggested, then glanced again at Jonas. "Er—whenever you have a chance."

"I will," Alexa told the maid.

Jonas quickly stepped up to them. "Don't let me interrupt, Alexa. I've got to get back to the men."

Alexa nodded at him. "I'll see you later tonight, Jonas."

Jonas hurried out of the house and didn't stop moving until he'd crossed the ranch yard and entered his office.

Inside the stark, dusty room he quickly plucked his cell phone from his shirt pocket, while telling himself he was getting too familiar with Alexa. All that talk about home and seeing him later. He'd heard those words before. They'd seemed nice and cozy and comfortable for a while. But it hadn't taken long for all that to change. No woman, not even one as special as Alexa, should make him forget that. Though he thought about a family, he wasn't ready to settle down now— or maybe ever.

He punched in the number that rang straight through to his captain and waited for the man to answer. Five minutes later, after he'd related Picken's tale about the cut fence, he ended the call. At that very moment, the door to his office opened, and the foreman over the ranch's remuda walked in.

Laramie Jones was nearing thirty, a quiet man who was wise beyond his years. The story went that he'd been a foster child, raised by an old ranch hand who'd worked on a spread in the Hondo Valley. He'd died when Laramie was only seventeen. That was when Lewis Cantrell had hired the young man on as a day hand. Thirteen years later Laramie made every important decision there was to be made about each and every horse on the Chaparral.

When Jonas's captain had approached Quint about hiring a Texas Ranger, Quint had already been planning to give the general manager position to Laramie. So Jonas had taken the job knowing that once the rustling case was wrapped up, he'd hand the reins of the ranch over to Laramie. And as far as Jonas could see, the other man clearly deserved the job.

"Am I interrupting?" Laramie asked.

Jonas motioned for him to take a seat. "Not in the least. What's going on? Trouble I need to know about?"

Laramie shook his head. "Nothing serious. One of the men took a spill this afternoon while they were moving cattle. He's okay, but one of my best geldings is now lame. I've called the vet, and he should be here shortly."

"Sometimes these things can't be helped. Let's hope the vet can take care of it," Jonas told the younger man. "Actually, I'm glad you stopped by. Two ton of new horse feed is going to be delivered later this afternoon. We'll talk about that stuff later and whether you think it will work out. Right now I wanted to ask you if you happen to be acquainted with Tyler Pickens?" He moved to sit down.

A slight grimace touched the other man's face. "Not well. He's not too friendly a character."

Leaning forward, Jonas propped his elbows on the desk. "I've already gathered that much. What I want to know is, is he an honest man?"

Laramie shrugged. "Never known him to get involved in double dealings or anything like that. Why?"

Jonas stroked his chin with his thumb and forefinger. "Nothing really. I met him today and we didn't exactly hit it off."

Laramie gave him a lopsided grin. "I'd be worried if you'd made fast friends with the man." He rose to his feet. "I really came by to say I've taken inventory, and we're going to need at least thirty more ton of alfalfa for the horses. I've put in a few calls to see where we might find the best price."

With a shake of his head, Jonas said, "Forget the price. I'm hearing the drought has cut the crop in half this year. Get it wherever you can find it. Quint won't quibble about the cost."

Laramie lifted the felt hat from his head and ran a hand through his dark hair. "You're right. I just like to cut corners if I can."

A truck and trailer rattled past the office, and the foreman glanced out one of the grimy windows. "There's the vet. I'd better go."

Jonas watched the man go out the door, then rose from his desk and walked over to the nearest window. But instead of peering down the ranch yard at the cattle pens and the never-ending activity around the barns, he gazed at the house.

From this angle he could see the long balcony attached to the upstairs bedrooms. Huge pots of red and fuchsia geraniums sat at intervals along the balustrade, while bent willow furniture with plush cushions was carefully grouped for relaxation.

The door to Alexa's bedroom was open,

but she wasn't on the balcony. He wondered if after he'd left the house, she'd gone upstairs to lie down or speak to her mother in private.

Damn it. It wasn't enough that he spent most of his nights lying awake, imagining her in the room next to his, he thought with a bit of self-disgust. Now he was taken to wondering about her in the light of day.

He'd definitely made a mistake by asking her to join him on the trip into town today, he decided. Still, he wouldn't take it back or change it, even if he could. He'd enjoyed the time with her too much. And a man had to derive some joy out of life. Especially when he'd gone for so long with so little.

Even so, just to be on the safe side, he wasn't going to see her tonight. He was going to make sure she was tucked safely away in her bedroom before he ever stepped foot in the house.

Much later that night Jonas was back in Ruidoso, sitting on a bar stool pretending to drink, while the men around him tossed down alcohol and talked about their day's work.

Since taking on the rustling case, Jonas had hit at least five different bars plus a nightclub over at Ruidoso Downs. The drinking spots were the perfect place to pick up information. But so far he'd not heard anything that might be connected to the Corriente cattle or to those who might be unlawfully hauling the coveted bulls and heifers into the country.

Tonight he was batting another zero. For the past two hours he'd sat munching pretzels, sipping warm beer and eavesdropping on stories about unruly kids, cheating wives, arrogant bosses and overly dramatized hunting expeditions.

Deciding he'd heard enough, he paid his tab and left the drinking establishment, all the while asking himself if he should make a call to Tyler Pickens tomorrow. The man had said he'd contact Jonas about showing him where the fence had been downed, but Jonas knew he might have to wait for days for the other man to get back to him. As Pickens had said, ranchers were busy men, and he didn't view the incident as a major crime. No doubt the rancher would shove the whole thing to the back burner.

The idea brought a tired sigh from Jonas as he climbed into his truck and started the engine. Presently the case was at a standstill. He needed to make things happen. Otherwise, it was going to be weeks before he saw Texas again. Weeks of dealing with Alexa Cantrell and the strange feelings she evoked in him.

The hands on his watch were nearing eleven-thirty by the time he returned to the ranch. As he parked in the back and made his way through the yard, he could see one dim light was burning in the kitchen. Alexa or the maid had probably left it on for him, and he was grateful for the gesture. Especially since he was still learning the layout of the house.

He was thinking he might slap some cold cuts between two slices of bread and eat the sandwich on his way up to bed as he stepped onto the back patio, but then he halted in his tracks.

There, lying on one of the cushioned loungers, was Alexa sound asleep. Her head was tilted to one side; her black hair spilled about her shoulders. A paperback book had slipped from her hand and fallen onto the concrete patio.

Jonas stooped and picked it up, then stared down at the sleeping goddess. What was she doing out here at such a late hour? Waiting on him? Oh God, he couldn't think that. No. He didn't want that from this woman. He'd had that from Celia, and he'd disappointed her time after time. The last thing he wanted to do was disappoint Alexa.

And yet to think that she might have been waiting to see him, speak with him, left his throat tight and a strange sensation swelling within his chest.

Trying his best to swallow the emotions, he bent down and softly touched a finger to her cheek. "Alexa. Wake up."

She stirred slowly, and then her blue eyes focused on his face. "Jonas! Where—" She broke off as she glanced around her. "Oh—I must have fallen asleep."

"It's going on midnight. You should be in bed."

She pushed herself into a sitting position, and Jonas straightened away from her.

"I—yes, I should. I was waiting on you to show up for supper." Her sleepy gaze slanted up at him. "What happened?"

He felt awful and guilty. Just like a thousand times before. "I had to go into town again for something."

He should have told her he'd be gone this evening. But he'd deliberately avoided doing that, too. Letting her in on his personal comings and goings would make it seem like she was important to him. Like they were a couple. He didn't want to give her the wrong idea. And yet he didn't want to hurt her. He wanted to scoop her up in his arms and kiss her. He wanted to tell her exactly what she was doing to him and show her exactly what he wanted to do with her. Lord was he confused!

She started to rise from the lounger, and Jonas reached a hand down to help her.

As she curled her fingers around his, she said, "You could have warned me you'd be gone."

"I'm sorry. I didn't think it mattered."

Standing next to him, she glanced up at his face, and for a moment Jonas thought he saw a flash of disappointment in her eyes. But he could have been wrong. Hell, he hoped he was wrong. Didn't he?

"Forget it," she said softly. Then, with her fingers still curled around his, she urged him toward the house. "Come on. There's food waiting for you on the stove."

As they entered the atrium and then the kitchen, Jonas told himself he should plead lack of hunger. He should say good-night and head straight up to his room. But he couldn't. He couldn't even find the strength to pull his hand away from hers.

Thankfully, she did that for him as she motioned for him to take a seat at the table, then stepped away to the cookstove.

"It's actually too late to eat," he said belatedly as he eased onto one of the dining chairs.

"You can't go to bed hungry, and we only had casserole tonight. This is no problem," she assured him.

While she waited for the food to heat up in the microwave, she placed a glass of tea on the table in front of him. Jonas couldn't help but notice she'd changed into a soft blue dress that pleated above her breast and draped demurely over her belly. As she moved about the kitchen, the fabric caressed her hips the same way his hands wanted to, and he wondered if he was becoming a pervert. Was it right to want a pregnant woman this much? he wondered with self-disgust.

The food turned out to be something with lots of green chilies and longhorn cheese. She'd placed a small basket of corn tortilla chips next to his plate, and he used the crispy chips to scoop up the meat concoction. Going to bed after eating such spicy food would probably keep him awake, but that wouldn't matter, he thought wryly. He'd hardly slept since moving into the house. Because Alexa was in the room next to his.

"Was everything okay with your mother?" he asked as she settled into a chair across from him.

A half smile touched her lips. "She's having the time of her life. One son has two children, and the other son is expecting a child in the fall. She's excited about getting to know her grandchildren."

His eyes settled on her. "And she has yours to look forward to, also. Is she planning to be back for the birth?"

"Oh, yes. She'll be home in about two weeks. I've told her to stay and enjoy herself as long as she can. There will be plenty of time for her to be with me and the baby later."

"Have you met your half brothers?" he asked.

She nodded. "Mac and Ripp spent some time here in the winter, when Mother had heart surgery. Mac even married a friend of the family—the doctor who was caring for my mother. I like them both. They're nice, respectable men. Both of them are deputy sheriffs. Seems being a lawman runs in their family."

Just like being a lawman ran in his, Jonas thought with a touch of sadness. The profession had killed his father, and it had ruined Jonas's marriage. What else was it going to do to him? Leave him a lonely bachelor without anything to show for his life? Still, it seemed that some men could make it work. God, he didn't want to think about that now.

Across the table he heard her draw in a long breath, then slowly release it.

"To be honest, Jonas, when I first met the two men I didn't exactly know what to feel about them. You see, it was shocking for me and my brother to learn that our mother had a family back in Texas. None of us had known about it. Except for our father. And he went to his grave without giving the secret away."

"Do you resent your half brothers appearing after all this time?"

Alexa shook her head. "Not exactly. I think I actually like the idea of having more brothers, and I believe I'll grow close to them. It's just the idea of my mother being someone else—something different than what I always believed. That shook me, Jonas. Do you understand what I mean?"

He looked down at his plate. "Yeah. Finding out someone isn't what you believed they were is always hard."

"She had a good reason for the choices she made," Alexa went on. "And I've forgiven her for keeping secrets. God knows, life is too short to waste time on anger—especially with your family."

For a long time Jonas had been angry about his father's death. He'd resented the townsfolk and blamed them for Curtis Redman's death. The mayor, the town council, every citizen should have made sure that there were adequate police officers to keep the town safe and secure. Instead, they'd piled the responsibility onto his father's shoulders until he crumbled. Now that years had passed and Jonas could look at it without so much pain in his heart, he realized that his father had been a grown man with the ability to make his own choices. He could have walked away. Instead, he'd died doing what he wanted to do. And that was about all a man could really ask for.

He gave her a brief smile. "Your mother is very lucky to have a daughter like you."

Her features softened, and then she surprised him by reaching over and laying her hand on his forearm. "That's a very nice thing to say, Jonas."

Hell, why did she have to be so sweet? Why wasn't she ranting and railing about him being out so late? Why wasn't she demanding to know where he'd been and what he'd been doing? Why did she have to talk about forgiveness and understanding, the traits he so often admired in the people who could truly practice them?

"Don't mistake me for a nice guy, Alexa. I'm really a selfish bastard when you get to know me."

Instead of his words putting her off, she merely chuckled as she slowly rose to her feet. "What are you going to do? Leave your dirty dishes on the table? Well, that wouldn't bother me. You've been working hard. You're entitled."

Jonas's brows lifted. "How do you know I've been working?"

Her hands curved over the back of the chair as she stood surveying him with dark blue eyes. "Haven't you?"

He hesitated for only a few seconds. "Sort of."

"What does that mean?" she asked as he stood and carried his dirty plate over to the counter.

Jonas decided to be as honest as he could with her. "Well, actually it means I spent most of this evening in a bar."

She laughed again, surprising him even more.

"That's supposed to be work?"

He grimaced as he carried the tea glass and basket of chips over to the spot where he'd left his plate. "It is when you don't want to be there."

She frowned. "Then why were you?"

He sighed as he walked over to where she stood in the middle of the room. "I was thinking—well, that I might overhear talk about the incident with Pickens's fence."

Confusion furrowed her brow. "Are you kidding? Why would anyone be talking about that? Things like that happen all the time. Fences get knocked down. Cattle stray onto other ranches, and the herds get mixed. Why would you even want to hear someone talking about that? It doesn't make sense."

No. It wouldn't make sense to her. Not without knowing what he knew. Taking her by the arm, Jonas asked, "Are you ready to go upstairs?"

She nodded. Then, as they headed out of the room, she said, "You didn't answer my question about Ty Pickens."

"I just don't like him accusing my men of destroying property, that's all. I'd like to know what really happened so I can throw the truth back in his face."

"Oh. Well, you're not going to find the an-

swer in a bar. I'm inclined to think some teenagers did it just as a prank. They probably
thought it funny that a few cowboys had to
work extra hours to separate a bunch of cattle."

"Why would teenagers be back in the
mountains?"

Turning her head toward his, she gave him
a droll look. "You have to ask? A boy, a girl,
a secluded place."

By now they'd reached the stairs, and as
Jonas curved his arm around the back of her
waist, he felt a flush of heat crawl up his face.
For some reason she had the ability to make
him feel very young and very old at the same
time.

"Hmm. That reason."

She didn't reply, but he could see that the
corners of her lips were tilted upward in a coy
fashion. The idea that she was flirting with
him in a vague sort of way had his fingers
tightening on the side of her waist and his hip
moving close enough to touch hers.

"I'm glad to learn you're not *that* dead,"
she said as they slowly climbed toward the
landing and the bedrooms beyond.

She smelled like flowers growing in green,
green grass, and everything about her felt soft
and precious. He wanted to keep touching

her, holding her next to him, pretending that she was his.

Before he could stop himself, he slowed his steps and then urged her to face him. He noticed her brows were arched in a questioning manner, but he didn't bother to register anything else as he bent his head and nuzzled his face against the side of her neck.

"I've never felt more alive in my life," he murmured. Then, placing a soft kiss beneath her ear, he brought his arms around her shoulders, gathered her closer and whispered, "Let me see how good you feel, taste."

Her groan was a sound of surrender, and he turned his head to rest the tip of his nose against hers. Her breaths were coming in rapid spurts, and he realized with a bit of surprise that his touching her was exciting her as much as it was him.

Tilting his head, he slanted his lips gently over hers and was instantly overcome by their velvety texture, the sweetness that spilled from them as she opened her mouth and returned his kiss.

Long, long moments went by before he finally broke the contact of their lips and lifted his head. He'd severed the connection only because he'd felt himself slipping toward a place he shouldn't be going.

"Oh, Jonas," she whispered, with dismay. "I'm huge and unattractive. And—"

"You're very beautiful, Alexa," he interrupted. His fingertips caressed the side of her cheek; then his palm gently rested upon the curve of her belly. "And the baby makes you even more beautiful."

As she gazed up at him, her eyes suddenly sparkled with tears and then, before he realized what was happening, she twisted out of his arms and hurried up the last few steps without him.

Stunned, Jonas stared after her for a moment. What had he done? Said?

Bounding after her, he caught up to her just as she was about to enter her bedroom. Capturing her by the hand, he tugged her back to him.

"Alexa! You're crying! What's wrong? If I hurt you, I'm sorry."

Her face was a picture of torn emotions as she stared up at him with eyes that were apologetic, pleading, sorrowful.

"You—you didn't do anything wrong, Jonas. It's just that—I've not heard anything so nice from a man in a long, long time."

Jonas's head was twisting back and forth even before he realized it. "Then why are you crying?"

More tears spilled over the rims of her eyes, and it was all Jonas could do to keep from pulling her into his arms, stroking her hair and promising her all the things he'd vowed to never again promise a woman.

"Because I can't do anything about it. Because I wish I'd met you a long time ago. I wish I'd never left this ranch in the first place. I wish too many things! Things that can never come true!"

Totally perplexed, he stared at her. What could he do or say to make it all better for her?

Hell, Jonas, you can't make it all better for Alexa. She needs a man who puts on a tie every morning and sits down at the dinner table promptly every night.

"Alexa, I—"

Suddenly she rose on her tiptoes and kissed his cheek. "Don't worry about me, Jonas. I'm just a woman about to have a baby. That's all. Forget everything I said. Please!"

Before he could make any sort of coherent reply, she pulled away from him and slipped behind her bedroom door.

Dazed, Jonas stood staring at the wooden panel, longing to open it and go after her, but knowing the best thing he could do was walk away.

I'm just a woman about to have a baby.

And he was a fool, reaching for something he could never have.

Chapter Five

Three days later, after a checkup with her doctor, Alexa drove out to Ruidoso Downs, where her friend Laurel Stanton worked at the Lincoln Animal Hospital. It was a veterinarian's office that mostly worked on horses that were raced on the nearby track, but the prominent doctor also treated cattle and smaller animals.

When she entered the office and inquired about her friend, the receptionist, an older woman with graying hair and a gentle smile, motioned to a door directly behind her.

"Laurel is back there with the cats. Go on in. You won't be interrupting anyone. The doctor is gone for the rest of the day, and Laurel is doling out medication."

"Thank you," she told the woman.

Behind the door was a long, wide hallway that opened on to examining rooms, and farther down was a ward of sorts, where caged animals recuperated from surgeries and illnesses. She found her friend here, among the hissing and the loud, soulful meows of the cats.

"Need any help?" Alexa called out as she stepped into the room.

The tall, chestnut-haired woman whirled around, then gasped with pleasure when she spotted Alexa.

"All that I can get!" Hurrying over, she hugged her friend close and laughed. "What are you doing here? Gosh, it's wonderful to see you! Finally!"

Since Alexa had returned to the Chaparral, she'd only had a chance to speak with Laurel on the phone. While Alexa had lived in Santa Fe, the two had kept in close contact, but today was the first time she'd seen her old friend in nearly two years.

"I just had a checkup at the clinic, and I thought I would stop by and see if we could talk for just a minute," Alexa told her. She stepped back and gave the other woman a thorough looking over. "You look great! You're so lean and tan and pretty! Doctoring animals must agree with you."

Laurel gestured toward the assortment of cats, two of which were walking in and out of her legs. "These are my babies," she said, with a fond grin. "So when is yours coming?"

"Probably not for four weeks. At least, that's when the due date is. The doctor says first babies are usually never on time, and though the baby is in position, he can't tell me a definite date. As for me, I'm ready any time."

"I'll just bet you are." Laurel looped her arm through Alexa's and urged her toward the door. "Come on. I'm finished in here. Let's take a break. I have a little cubbyhole of an office just down the hall."

Laurel led her to the small room, then shut the door behind them. As she gestured for Alexa to take a seat in a cushioned wicker chair, she walked over to a tiny fridge and pulled out two bottles of fruit juice.

"Doc is out on call. He won't be back for the rest of the day." She handed one of the bottles to Alexa. "He irks the hell out of me at times, leaving me to deal with all this work by myself, but I love the animals, so I put up with him."

She sat down in a chair facing Alexa and twisted the lid off the glass bottle. Alexa smiled as she watched her friend tilt the drink to her lips.

"It's so good to see you, Laurel. It seems... well, seeing you makes me feel like I'm really home again."

"For good this time?" Laurel asked.

Alexa's gaze dropped to her lap. "Probably. I don't know. I hate giving up my job, but Barry has ruined it for me. I don't think I'd ever be happy working there again. Seeing him most every day would only remind me of what an idiot I was."

Laurel shook her head. "Why are you still being so hard on yourself? I've had relationships with several stinkers, and I never thought I should go jump off a cliff because I made bad choices."

Alexa grimaced. "I never wanted to jump off a cliff."

"No. But you thought the world had come to an end."

A radio was playing on a small, cluttered desk behind them. The country music made her think of Jonas. But then, these days everything made her think of Jonas.

"Laurel, I'm pregnant with the man's child. And he's—he turned out to be a real creep."

"You didn't know that when the baby was conceived."

"That's exactly why I was so upset when I discovered the hidden side of Barry. I *should* have known it. But I didn't come here to talk about that. How are your parents?"

"Good. Mom got a job over at the track, doing office work. So far she loves it. And Dad had a health scare for a few days last month, but that turned out to be nothing. So how is your mother? Counting the days until you give birth to her grandchild, I'm sure."

"She's gone to Texas right now to visit my half brothers. And Quint is still staying at the ranch house he's renovating, so I've basically been alone for the past two weeks."

Laurel frowned. "I can't believe your family is allowing you to stay in that huge house alone. Anything could happen to you! Maybe I should come stay with you until your mother gets back."

Sighing, Alexa twisted the cap off the bottle of fruit juice. "I'm not alone, Laurel. Sassy is there, and Jonas is there at night."

Her brows arched, Laurel looked at her. "Jonas? Do I know him?"

Alexa shook her head. "I doubt it. He's the new general manager that Quint hired several weeks ago. He's from Texas. San Antonio to be exact."

"Hmm. Must be a trustworthy man for your family to want him staying in the house with you."

"He's a complete gentleman."

The toe of Laurel's cowboy boot tapped the air as she studied Alexa closely. "I hear fondness in your voice, Alexa. Tell me about this man."

Alexa could feel her cheeks turning red, and it had nothing to do with vacillating hormones or the heat of the day. "There's nothing to tell. He's good-looking and intelligent and polite and—"

Laurel smiled knowingly. "And you like him. A lot."

Alexa nodded.

"Good! This is the best news I've heard from you in months!"

Rising to her feet, Alexa began to meander aimlessly around the small room. "You think so? I think I'm acting like an idiot. Again."

"Why?"

Groaning, Alexa thrust a hand through her wavy hair. "Laurel, I'm in no condition to be looking at a man in—well—*that* way. But there's something about him that I just can't seem to resist. God knows, you've heard me say time and time again that I'd never fall for another cowboy, but this one is—"

"Different? Special?" Laurel finished for her.

"Yes," Alexa answered sheepishly, then groaned again. "Oh, Laurel, I think—I'm afraid I'm falling in love with the man!"

"So what's so terrible about that?" Laurel wanted to know. "He certainly sounds like a wonderful dream compared to that stuffed shirt you had in Santa Fe. Finally, finally, it sounds like you're coming to your senses and looking at a man that's right for you."

"I wouldn't be so quick to say that." Alexa rested her hip on one corner of the desk. An arm's length away sat a framed picture of Laurel's twin sister, who died at the age of twelve. The photo reminded Alexa that she hardly owned the market on heartache. Laurel and her family had been dealt plenty of their own.

Her friend said, "I suppose there's an explanation for that doubt crawling across your face."

Groaning, Alexa replied, "Look, Laurel, Jonas has already been married once. That turned out badly, and he's said in not so many words that he doesn't want to repeat the experience. Besides that, I'm not so sure he's looking at me in the same way I'm looking at him."

Laurel chuckled. "Is this cowboy blind?"

Alexa rolled her eyes and patted her rotund waistline. "My dear friend, do I look like I could attract a man?" She glanced down at the bottle she was gripping with both hands. "Besides," she added somberly, "I'm about to be a single mother. Lots of men aren't willing to take on a ready-made family."

"If that's the way this Jonas thinks, then he isn't worth the energy it would take to kick his backside." Leaning forward, Laurel bent her head in an attempt to peer up at Alexa's lowered face. "Is that really the sort of man he is?"

Funny, but Alexa didn't have to wonder about Laurel's question. Somehow, without even asking, she knew that if Jonas loved a woman, he would love her child just as much. The real question was how did he feel about her. The kiss he'd given her the other night had clearly said he wanted her in a basic, physical way. But what about love?

Lord, what was she thinking? Just because the man had shown a slight bit of interest in her, she was letting her head go straight to the clouds. Jonas wasn't thinking about caring or love or the future. He was simply a man who'd wanted to kiss her. And that wasn't anything to get excited over.

But she was excited. She couldn't deny it. And that in itself worried her. She had the coming baby to think about. Her child had to be her first priority. Her feelings, her wants would have to come way down the list. In the past months, she had learned through her mother just exactly how much it cost a woman's heart to love the wrong man. Alexa couldn't let that happen this time.

"No. I don't believe Jonas would be that way. He seems interested in the baby. And he's always reminding me to take care of myself."

"Does he have any children of his own?"

Alexa shook her head. "No children. And I don't know what happened to his marriage. But I've never heard him bad-mouthing his ex-wife or blaming her."

"I know a few men who could take lessons from him," Laurel muttered.

Glancing up at her friend, Alexa smiled. "That's enough about me. I want to hear about what you've been doing. I can't remember the last time you told me you were going out on a date. And look at you—a beautiful woman going to waste."

Tilting her head back, Laurel laughed. "That's why you've always been my best friend, Alexa. You'd make me feel wonderful even if my head was cracking with a migraine." Her laughter subsiding, she shook her head. "No dates. When would I have time? Most weeknights I'm working overtime here at the clinic, and lots of weekends Doc calls me out to assist with emergencies."

"Hmm. Sounds as though nothing has changed with you. Your life revolves around this place. One of these days I'd like to meet this Doc and tell him it's time he let up on you."

Laurel grimaced. "Don't worry. I tell him that all the time. It doesn't help. But what the heck—the animals make me happy. They give me all the love I need, and they don't care if I'm looking my best or if I make mistakes. What more could a woman ask for?"

Plenty, Alexa thought. *Children, a home, a man to grow old with.* But she wasn't in any position to point that out to Laurel. She'd made too many mistakes to be giving advice to anyone.

"A good meal?" Alexa teased as she placed the nearly empty fruit-juice bottle on the desktop. "I'd love for you to come out one evening and have dinner with me. Reena's cooking is so scrumptious, I'm having a hard time resisting seconds. The baby must be packing on the fat. I stay hungry all the time."

"Ha! I stay hungry all the time, and I'm only eating for myself," Laurel joked. "But I'll try my best to make it out one evening. It's been ages since I've seen the Chaparral."

Rising to her feet, Alexa stepped over and kissed Laurel's cheek. "I'm going to hold you to it. Right now, I'd better go. It's getting late, and it's a long drive back to the ranch."

With a good-natured groan, Laurel left her chair. "Okay. Since you're forcing me back to work, I'll walk with you to your car."

That night Alexa didn't see Jonas. She'd hung around downstairs, hoping he'd show before her eyes got too heavy, and when he didn't, she'd told herself she was behaving like a lovesick heifer and gone to bed.

But this morning she woke earlier than usual, and when she stepped out into the hallway, she spotted him walking toward the staircase landing. It was the first time she'd encountered him since their kiss, and though she'd been longing to be close to him again, she couldn't help but feel a bit of embarrassment for shedding tears in front of the man.

"Good morning, Jonas."

At the sound of her voice, he turned, and as she looked at him, attraction whammed her like a fist. He was dressed all in denim this morning, and a straw cowboy hat was tilted low on his forehead. His body was a walking mass of lean muscle; his face raw and tough. Every inch of him was all man, and every inch of her reacted to him in the most erotic way.

"Alexa! You're up very early. It's not yet daylight."

She moved toward him. "I went to bed early. Do you have time for coffee? I have something to ask you."

He glanced at his watch. "The men are saddling up right about now. I suppose they can do without me for another five minutes."

Smiling, she reached his side, and the tender look in his eyes was like a warm hand touching her on a cold night. The awkwardness she'd felt a moment ago swiftly fled as she looped her arm through his and they started down the staircase together.

He smelled of simple soap and some musky scent that belonged uniquely to him. Being near him was like stepping into a candy store. She wanted to touch and taste, peel off the outside and enjoy the gooey goodness inside.

"How was your doctor's visit yesterday? Is the baby okay?" he asked as they descended the stairs.

She glanced at him with surprise. "How did you know I had a doctor's visit?"

"You told me on our ride to town."

His concern touched her. Yet she told herself that he would be just as concerned over any pregnant woman in his presence.

"The baby and I are both fine. Just ticking off the days until he or she gets here."

"Are you prepared for that?" he asked, then quickly added, "I mean, do you have a crib and bottles and all those sorts of things ready?"

"As soon as Mother learned I was expecting, she went to work on a nursery. It's in a smaller room that connects to my bedroom. As for the bottles—" she chuckled softly "—this little guy of mine is going to eat naturally."

From the corner of her eye, Alexa could see a hint of red color seep into his face. It was refreshing to see a man with a bit of modesty, she thought. Especially compared to the ribald comments Barry and his friends had made about women breast-feeding. Strange how she'd not noticed how crude he and his buddies had been when they'd first learned of her pregnancy. Or maybe she had noticed their behavior but had simply overlooked it to make herself fit in the crowd. Trouble was, nothing about that political, social crowd had been right for her. She'd been trying to fit into something that was the wrong shape and size to suit her. And she should have realized that about herself long before she'd taken a serious look at Barry.

Jonas said, "It sounds like you intend to take extra special care of the little fellow."

Her heart softened as she once again glanced his way. "I'm going to try my best."

Once they entered the kitchen, Alexa forced herself to release her hold on his arm just as Reena turned away from the cookstove.

In her quiet way, the cook nodded her good

morning, then went back to stirring a skillet full of sizzling chorizo sausage.

"I'll get the coffee," Jonas told her.

Alexa took her seat at the kitchen table, then thanked him as he served her a mug full of coffee with a heavy dose of cream.

As for Jonas, he stood, his hip leaning against the edge of the table, as he carefully sipped the steaming java. "So you needed to speak with me this morning?"

There was something about having his eyes on her that made Alexa feel naked, even though she was decently covered with a white cotton robe. The idea left her uncomfortably warm, and without even realizing it, she allowed her gaze to settle on his hard lips. Her mind spun back to the moment he'd pressed them against hers.

"Uh—" She cleared her throat, then swallowed. "Yes. But don't look so concerned. There's no problem. I actually—well, I wanted to ask you on an outing with me. That is, if you'd like to go."

His eyes widened just a fraction. "What sort of outing?"

She laughed at the wariness in his voice. "Don't worry, Jonas. I'm not going to pull you into a roomful of giggling women. I wanted to take you to meet my grandfather this evening and have supper with him. I called him last night and asked him about it. He's very anxious to meet you."

He studied her for long moments. "I can't believe your grandfather wants to meet me. But I appreciate his hospitality. Sure. I'll go. There's nothing going on today that should keep me working late."

It was crazy how much joy was suddenly spilling through her. And though she recognized the foolishness of her reaction, she refused to squash her happiness.

"Great! I'll be ready to go around four. I know that sounds early, but it's a bit of a drive, and I want to show you around the place before it gets dark."

"Fine. I'll see you at four." He placed his mug on the table, then turned and tipped the brim of his hat at Reena. "Thanks for the coffee, ma'am."

Smiling slightly, the cook nodded back at him. Then, after he disappeared out the back door, she looked over to Alexa. "You're taking him to meet Abe?"

Alexa nodded. Then, noticing the cook's sober expression, she asked, "Why? You think that's a bad idea?"

"No. It just surprises me. That's all."

Alexa stared down at the coffee swirling in her mug. "Because he's a cowboy. Because after Mitch—"

"You've gotten over that, Alexa. And this man is different. He's responsible."

Yeah, he was responsible, Alexa thought. But he wasn't accountable for her happiness. She had to depend on herself for that, and so far she'd been making a mess of things. But she wasn't going to dwell on all those mistakes this morning. She was going to think about Jonas and the evening to come.

Rising to her feet, she walked over to where Reena stood working at the cookstove and peered over the woman's shoulder. "Is that sausage ready yet? I'm starving."

Jonas didn't know what he was doing accepting Alexa's invitation to supper. He tried to tell himself he could call the outing business. After all, old man Cantrell might have heard gossip about the Corriente cattle, and this would be a good way to subtly question him. But who was he kidding? He was thinking of the whole thing as a date. A date with a beautiful, desirable woman. And *she* had asked him. That made the whole thing even nicer.

At four o'clock that afternoon, he found Alexa in the living room, flipping through the channels on the television. As soon as she spotted him, she snapped the off button and rose to her feet.

"Oh my," she said as she took one long look at him. "You didn't have to dress up!"

He glanced down at his Western-cut khakis and blue striped shirt. "This isn't dressing up, but if you think it's too much, I'll go put on my jeans."

Shaking her head, she walked over to him. "Of course not. I just look like I'm ready for wash day." She gestured to the black jeans and white oversize shirt she was wearing. "But that's okay, because we're going to do a bit of climbing."

"Climbing?" he asked, with dismay. "Are you in any condition to do any climbing?"

They both moved toward the door, and Jonas held it open so that she could pass through first.

"It's nothing rough or steep. I promise. Just a nice walk."

"I'm certainly going to make sure of that," he assured her.

The drive to Abe Cantrell's ranch, Apache Wells, took a little over forty minutes. Situated to the north and west, toward Carrizozo, the homesite was nestled in a network of foothills just east of the White Mountain Wilderness area. As they approached the house itself, Alexa informed him that the property ran for so many miles that part of it extended beyond the mountains and into flat desert land, where cattle had to hunt for blades of grass behind rocks and cholla cacti.

As they crawled up a narrow, graveled drive, Jonas could see that the ranch house was nothing like the grand hacienda-style house at the Chaparral. It was a modest home built of a mixture of rough cedar and stucco. Huge pines hugged its walls and sheltered the tin roof, which sloped steeply toward the ground. A wooden sidewalk curved toward a small sheltered portico. A black-and-white collie was lying at the foot of the screen door, but she quickly jumped to her feet and barked when she saw them approach.

"If you don't mind my asking, why did your father move away from here and build the Chaparral?" Jonas asked as he braked the truck to a halt. "Seems like he would have stayed on here to help his father run Apache Wells."

Alexa shrugged. "For a while, after my father became a grown man, he did stay on here at Apache Wells. But Gramps is—well, I guess you'd call him a land baron. He owns land scattered all over Lincoln County, and he eventually put my father to work building another ranch. I guess Gramps intuitively understood that someday Lewis would want a place of his own. Just like he understands that Quint needs a special place to call his own. That's why he's put him to work building the Golden Spur," she explained.

"This is a nice place," Jonas said after he helped Alexa to the ground. "Nice and quiet and private."

"The ranch is very secluded, but Gramps likes it that way. I'm not so sure Granny liked being away from everything and everyone, but while she was still living she had lots of friends over, and that made up for the isolation, I suppose." Grabbing his hand, she urged him forward. "Come along and we'll find my grandfather."

"Where is the working part of the ranch?" he asked, curious. "The barns and everything?"

"Two miles straight back behind the house. Granny made him build that part of the ranch away from the house. She didn't want dust covering everything." Alexa laughed. "And believe me, whatever she wanted, she got."

"Must have been quite a woman," he murmured. *Kind of like you,* he wanted to add. He could see most any man breaking his back to give Alexa whatever her heart desired. Could he be that generous? Oh, yes, he would do his best to give her everything. Until it came to his job. That he wouldn't be able to put aside just to please her. He'd tried with Celia and it hadn't worked. Being a Ranger was a part of him. It was too important to him and the state of Texas. To take it away from him would be like hacking off a part of his body. And he'd not yet met a woman who understood that.

Before they reached the door, an older man with a head full of salt-and-pepper hair and a drooping white mustache stepped onto the small porch. He was as thin as a rail and was wearing faded jeans, with the legs stuffed into a pair of black-and-red bull-hide boots. A pair of Jingle Bob spurs tinkled as he stepped forward and held his arms out to Alexa.

"It's a hell of thing when my granddaughter is home for more 'n two weeks and is just now coming to see me."

Jonas could see tears filling Alexa's eyes as she hurried to the man and snuggled her face against his chest. "Go ahead and scold me, Gramps. I should have come sooner. But I knew you had Quint keeping an eye on you."

"An eye, my foot! That boy rarely shows his face around here."

Laughing, Alexa kissed the man's leathery cheek, then levered herself away from his chest. "That's because you've been keeping him so busy. What do you expect?"

"A little respect. That's what." His squinted eyes peered toward Jonas. "Is this the young fella you were tellin' me about?"

Smiling at both men, Alexa motioned for Jonas to join them. "This is him, Gramps."

She quickly introduced the two men, and Jonas gave the older man's hand a firm shake. "It's very nice to meet you, Mr. Cantrell. Your granddaughter speaks of you often."

Abe Cantrell smiled fondly at his granddaughter. "Rakin' me over the coals, I suppose. Tellin' you what a crotchety old codger I am."

"No, sir. She speaks of you fondly."

With a loud clearing of his throat, Abe gestured toward the door. "Well, let's don't just stand out here like we don't have good sense. Jim has everything cooked and ready. Lamb chops. Sent him after them just this mornin'."

"Is Jim still here?" Alexa asked of the ranch's longtime cook.

"Nope. He's twenty years younger than me, but he thinks he has to hurry back to the bunkhouse and beat the rest of the guys to his recliner. Damn man. He complains about his arthritis, but what in hell will he be like when he gets to be my age?"

"Nothing like you, Gramps," Alexa said, then winked covertly at Jonas as the three of them entered the house.

Everything inside was old and comfortable, and Jonas felt completely at home as the three of them sat in the living room while he and Abe sipped beer and Alexa had a small glass of ginger ale.

They talked for at least thirty minutes before Abe decided it was time to eat. The cook had left everything in a warming drawer in the bottom of the stove, and in spite of the old man trying to shoo her into a chair, Alexa insisted on putting the food out on the table. Jonas made a point to help her; all the while he could feel the old man watching him and his granddaughter.

No doubt wondering about the connection between them, Jonas figured. But he could have assured the old man there was no connection. At least not anything more than liking and respect.

Liar, liar. You feel more than that for Alexa. That kiss you shared with her the other night has never left your mind. All you can think about is kissing her again.

Thankfully, Abe was never at a loss for words, and as they began to eat the hearty meal, the old man kept the conversation going and Jonas's mind off his need to be close to Alexa. Or, at least, partially off it. Most of the time his thoughts were vacillating between Abe's stories and the fact that Alexa was sitting only inches from his side.

"So why did you want your grandson to develop the land you own over toward Capitan?" Jonas asked him. "Is that something you've always wanted to do?"

Abe smoothed his thumb and forefinger over the ends of his mustache. "Not always. I thought it was high time the boy had other interests on his mind. Hell, the Chaparral has developed into a huge business. Now that you've taken over, he's not needed there."

Jonas wouldn't say that. Most days he was up to his neck in work. "So you plan to run cattle on this new ranch you're building?"

"Cattle and horses," Abe said with a confident nod. "I want to see it thrive before I die."

"Gramps! Don't talk that way. You're not going to die!" said Alexa.

With a dry look at his granddaughter, Abe shook his head. "Is that so? Well, that's news to me. I thought everyone died. Didn't know I was gonna escape that event."

"Gramps, you know what I mean," Alexa scolded him. "You're not going to die anytime soon. You're just like an old mule. Life doesn't wear you down."

Abe reached across the small table and patted her cheek. "Just the same, I want things like I want them before I meet my Maker. And I'm trying like hell to talk Quint into reopening the Golden Spur."

Alexa gasped so loudly that Jonas first thought a labor pain had struck her. "What's wrong?" he asked. "What's the Golden Spur?"

Her eyes were wide as they swung from Abe over to him. "It's an old mine that's sits on part of the property. A gold mine. It closed way back in the late eighteen hundreds."

"I didn't know there was ever gold in this area," said Jonas.

"Sure, boy," Abe asserted. "At one time, lots of it. Even had a railroad over by White Oaks. But when the gold dried up, it all became a ghost town. But some folks are still digging around these parts, and bits and pieces are being found."

There was a passion in the old man's voice, which told Jonas this was a subject that fascinated him. And not for the money that might be involved, but simply because of the adventure of it.

Alexa added, "There was even a mine called Old Abe in the area that Gramps is talking about. But it wasn't named for him. That was long before the turn of the last century."

"Hmm. That's interesting. So you think there might still be gold on your property?" Jonas asked Abe.

"I'm as sure of that as I am that the sun will rise in the east. 'Course, Quint ain't as confident as me. He thinks I'm frittering away a fortune. But hell, that's not the point. It's the idea of a man bein' productive, of makin' use of what God gave us."

"I didn't realize you'd been discussing such things," Alexa interjected. "Quint's not mentioned anything about the mine to me."

Abe settled a pointed look at her. "You've been gone. You ain't been a part of things for a long time."

For a moment she looked hurt, and Jonas instantly wanted to scold the old man for speaking to her in such a way, but then he saw a spark of anger light Alexa's eyes, and he realized she could defend herself.

"Well, you can forget that!" Alexa tossed hotly back at her grandfather. "I'm back now, and you're going to have to deal with me, too. And I'll tell you another thing, Gramps. I'm not nearly the pushover that Quint is!"

Abe appeared stunned for a moment, and then he began to cackle with joy and slap his hand down so hard on the table that the plates bounced. "Now, that's the girl I wanted to see come to my supper table! It's about time she showed up, instead of that whimpering little city girl you tried to be!" He rose from his chair and went around the table to kiss her cheek. "Welcome home, darlin'."

She looked at Jonas and smiled, and this

time the tears he saw in her eyes were tears of pride and joy. The sight made him feel far happier than he ever should. This woman and her family had nothing to do with him. He was here on a job. Nothing more. Nothing less.

Now make yourself remember that, Jonas.

Chapter Six

Long after the meal was eaten and the coffee drank, Alexa informed her grandfather that she was taking Jonas to see the springs. Jonas didn't know what she meant, and he didn't ask until she led him outside, beneath the pines.

"Just what are these springs? And are they close enough for you to walk?" he asked.

"The springs," she told him as she wrapped both hands around his left arm, "are natural springs of water that flow from a small mountain just over the rise that way. Not far." She pointed in a northerly direction. "That's where the ranch got its name. Legend goes that the Mescalero Apaches used to dwell here because of the abundance of water."

"Is that where the ranch gets its water today?"

She urged him forward. "Probably from the same vein. But these springs aren't piped. It's all natural. And very pretty there. I always like to hike up there whenever I come to see Gramps."

The walk to the springs didn't require any exertion on Jonas's part, but he worried about Alexa, and he made sure to keep his arm at the back of her waist at all times. By the time they'd wound their way through the pines and over the rocky trail that climbed to the springs, he could see she was winded, and he quickly made her sit on one of the flat rocks that surrounded a beautiful blue pool of water situated beneath the ledge of mountain.

"Wow! This is a special place," Jonas exclaimed as he eased down next to her. "I wasn't expecting anything like this."

"I'm sure this little oasis would surprise most people who aren't familiar with this part of the state. When Gramps first bought the property, he realized he had a gold mine right here in the water. That was way back in nineteen fifty-six. He came here from Texas, you know, when he was a very young man. So you two have something in common."

"You mean, besides you?"

She looked at him, and the soft smile tilting the corner of her lips made him groan inside. All the while they'd been walking, he'd been touching her, breathing in her sweet scent as the warmth of her body seeped into the palm of his hand and spread through his body like a rivulet of slowly inching lava. Now all he could think about was holding her close, feeling her lips pressed against his.

"Do you *have* me, Jonas?" she asked demurely.

"Not really. But I'd like to."

His words were all it took to draw her head toward his, and then everything exploded as Jonas's hand curved against the back of her neck and their mouths met.

The sound of the trickling water, the birds twittering in the limbs of the pines, the insects buzzing in nearby bushes couldn't drown out the sound of his heartbeat pounding loudly in his ears or the undoing moan coming from deep in her throat.

Fire seemed to lick between their lips, turning that slow-moving lava into raging flames racing straight to his loins.

With a needy groan, he pulled her closer, angling the top of her body across his lap and against his chest. At the same time his fingers dove into her thick hair and scrunched the soft black waves.

At some point he recognized her arms slipping around his neck, her breasts smashing against his chest. Beneath his elbow he could feel the mound of her belly, her baby. Logic tried to push into his brain, yet it couldn't break through the foggy desire swirling around him. In spite of everything, he found himself thinking of the child as his. His and hers. Theirs. The idea was euphoric to him, and it fueled his want for her even more.

Just as he deepened the kiss, she opened her mouth, pushing her tongue between his lips until the tip of it touched his teeth. He groaned deep in his throat as urgent need seemed to pluck up his insides and twist them into agonizing knots.

His tongue thrust forward to meet hers as his lips rocked back and forth, searching every curve and crevice, searching for the relief he needed. Unwittingly his hands slipped to the mounds of her breasts, while his heart pounded like an engine on the verge of exploding.

He didn't know which one of them finally broke the contact between their lips. Nor did it matter. As soon as they both gulped in several raspy breaths of air, their mouths were back together. Clinging, tasting, worshiping.

Her hands began to roam over his chest and back, scalding him with trails of excitement, and when he sensed her fingers fumbling with the buttons on his shirt, all he could think about was having her naked in his arms, of kissing every inch of her, of making long, hot love to her.

The drops of rain came slowly at first. Spattering here and there like birds hopping from one worm to the next. Jonas did his best to ignore them. He didn't want to relinquish the heaven in his arms. But after a few more moments, the drops began to gather into full-fledged rainfall, forcing them to rise to their feet and hurry away from the springs.

By the time they reached the shelter of the house, they were both soaked, and Alexa was laughing about her plastered hair and shirt. As for Jonas, even the cold raindrops had done little to put out the fire she'd started in him, and he wondered how long it would be before he slipped up and made love to her.

If Leo, his captain, knew what was going

on, he'd jerk Jonas out of New Mexico so fast, it would create a whirlwind large enough to tear up this whole ranch. But Alexa wasn't a part of the smuggling case, he reasoned. Being with her wasn't going to jeopardize his mission. Especially since she knew absolutely nothing about illegal cattle coming into the state, he continued to argue in his mind.

But she was going to have to be told. Of that much Jonas was certain. He couldn't go on like this. She deserved to know the real reason he was here in New Mexico and working on her ranch as much as he deserved the right to be honest with her.

If learning he was a Ranger ended their fledging relationship, then he'd know he'd done the right thing. No matter how much it hurt.

Chapter Seven

Inside Abe's cozy log house, the three of them watched the television screen with dismay. Not only was the local weatherman warning that a line of heavy rain was coming, but he was reporting widespread flooding just to the north of Lincoln County and moving south toward the Chaparral area.

Rising urgently to her feet, Alexa turned to her grandfather. "We'd better leave, Gramps. Or Jonas and I might not be able to cross the river."

Abe's concerned gaze included both of them. "Why don't you two stay here with me tonight?" he suggested. "I'd feel better knowing you're not drivin' through the mountains in this frog floater."

Alexa glanced at Jonas, and he could tell by the faint nuances of her expression that she preferred to be home in her own bed. Whether she wanted Jonas in that bed with her was a question he tried to push out of his mind.

"Jonas is a very good driver," she assured Abe. "Besides, I have all kinds of book work to catch up on tomorrow."

Jonas added, "And I have several things scheduled to do. I really need to get back to the Chaparral tonight."

The old man waved a dismissive hand at them. "Fine. Go ahead. You young people don't know how to use much common sense anyway," he muttered.

Alexa fetched her purse and the light jacket she'd brought with her, and they quickly said their goodbyes to Abe and left the house.

Even as they walked to the truck, the steady rain was growing harder, and by the time they drove off the Cantrell property and reached the main highway, it was pouring.

Nightfall had also come upon them, and the wet asphalt made seeing through the downpour even more tricky. Jonas adjusted the speed of the truck to a very slow pace and carefully guided the tires away from the deep puddles collecting on the rutted roadway.

They'd traveled only a few miles when Alexa's cell phone rang. The voice on the other end of the crackling connection was so dim, she could barely make it out.

"Sassy? Is that you?"

"Alexa!" Sassy shouted back at her. "I'm here—at my friend's house. The streets are flooding! I don't think I'd better try to drive home in this—tonight."

"No—no. I don't want you out in this," Alexa assured her. "Stay there and stay safe. I'll see you tomorrow."

"What about you? Are—things okay—? Where—?"

The phone went dead before Sassy could finish her questions. Alexa snapped the phone shut and glanced over at Jonas, who was keeping his gaze fastened on the wet highway in front of them.

"The weather must be doing something to the phone signal. Everything went dead. I guess it's just as well. I didn't want to tell Sassy we're on the highway. She would worry."

"Well, at this speed, it might take a while

to get home," he told her. "But we'll get there. I promise. Just lean back and try to relax."

More than an hour and a half later they were on Chaparral land, and Jonas braked the truck to a halt at the edge of the low water bridge that crossed the Bonito. Water was already running over the planked boards.

His expression was grim when he glanced over at her. "I don't like the idea of driving across this bridge. Not with you in the truck," he said.

She peered out at the wooden structure spanning the river. Rarely did the river spill out of its banks, but there had been a few times in the past when it had flooded. Before he died, Lewis had erected a safety gauge so that travelers could make out the depth of the water.

The beam of their headlights illuminated the railings that served as guard rails on each side of the wooden span. Leaning forward, Alexa strained to see the water markers.

"It's okay, Jonas," she finally said with relief. "Can you see the white lines painted on the left side of the bridge banister? Right now the water is only touching the bottom line. That means it's still safe to cross. Let's go!"

Jonas didn't argue with her. Being caught on

this side of the river in the middle of a fierce rainstorm was the last thing they needed. But thankfully the bridge was solidly intact, and the water was not yet high enough for the swift current to sweep them downriver.

A few minutes later they finally arrived at the house. Jonas parked the truck near the front steps and quickly helped Alexa into the living room.

A lamp was burning in a far corner of the room, and in the dim glow he glanced over to see her struggling to peel off the damp jacket she was wearing. There was a strained look of fatigue on her face, and he realized the harrowing trip back home had taken a toll on her.

"Let me help you with that," he murmured. "You look exhausted."

Standing behind her, he pulled the jacket from her shoulders, then tossed it over the back of a nearby chair.

"I am really tired," she admitted as she shoved strands of wet hair off her face. "I guess I've done too much today."

Back beside her, he rested his hands on her shoulders. "You shouldn't have taken me on that hike to the springs," he gently admonished.

A weary smile touched her lips, and he felt

his heart turn over with concern and love. *Love? No. Not that kind of love,* he quickly corrected himself. He cared about her. Yes. *Cared.* That was the right word.

"I wanted you to see it. It's one of my favorite places in the world, and you're the first person I've ever taken there."

Jonas tried to downplay the significance of her words. But that was hard to do when everything inside of him wanted this woman to admire him, want him.

He brushed his fingertips against her cheek. "Alexa, at the springs—when we kissed. I—hadn't planned on things getting so out of hand." Shaking his head, he searched for the right way to explain his torn emotions. "I want you to know that I—not for anything would I have hurt you. I mean, I wanted you—a lot. But you're going to have a baby and—"

Before he could say more, she touched her fingertips to his lips, and her eyes sparkled with moisture as they glided over his face. "Jonas," she whispered, "just because I'm pregnant doesn't mean I can't make love. At the springs—I wanted you, too. A lot. But now—" her lips curved into a regretful smile "—I'm afraid I'm a bit too tired to invite you into my bed tonight."

She'd barely gotten the words past her lips when she began to weave on her feet, then topple toward him.

"Dear God, Alexa!"

Catching her before she fell, Jonas lifted her into his arms and quickly carried her up the stairs and into her bedroom.

After he'd placed her on the bed, he helped her out of her rain-soaked shirt and jeans.

"Where's a nightgown?" he demanded. "I don't want you getting off that bed for any reason."

She told him where to find the garment, and once he returned to her with the piece of flimsy blue fabric, he helped her peel away her undergarments.

"I didn't want you to see me like this," she said with embarrassment as he lowered the nightgown over her head.

"Don't be silly," he said gently. "You look beautiful. Tired. But beautiful."

Glancing up at him, she tried to laugh. "You have the tired part right." Reaching for his hand, she clasped her fingers around his. "And I'm sorry, but I do have to leave the bed for one thing. The bathroom. If you'll just help me, I promise I'll get right back in bed."

"I'm here to help," he softly assured her.

"No. You're here to manage the ranch. You didn't know you were going to become my nursemaid." She glanced at him with a bit of wry regret as he helped her back to her feet. "I'm so sorry I said that to you, Jonas. I was such a crab to you that day. You must have been thinking awful things about me. And I wouldn't have blamed you."

He'd been thinking a lot of things that day, Jonas thought. But none of them could compare to the thoughts running through his head right now. The feel of this woman he held in the circle of his arms was far more precious than he'd ever expected it to be.

"We all have our days, Alexa. And I forgot all that a long time ago."

She was in the bathroom only a few short minutes. Jonas helped her back to the bed; then, because the air had grown chilly, he pulled the covers up to her chin.

Outside the rain was still pouring down, and every now and then bolts of lightning streaked across the sky and flashed in the bedroom. By the time he switched off the lamp at the head of the bed and leaned down to kiss her forehead, her eyes had already drifted shut.

"I'll be right in the next room if you need me," he whispered.

Inside his own bedroom, he switched on the radio for a weather report. While he waited for the top-of-the-hour newscast, he flipped open his cell phone and saw that he'd missed two calls. Laramie had called less than an hour ago. But the surprise was the name below his. Tyler Pickens.

Hell! Jonas had been waiting for days now to hear from the man, and he decided to call on a night like this!

Glancing at his watch, he realized it was far too late to call Pickens, but Laramie wouldn't mind if he interrupted his evening. Especially if there'd been a problem while Jonas had been away from the ranch.

When he punched in the foreman's number, the phone's ring was erratic, and he didn't expect the call to get through. Jonas was about to end the connection entirely when the other man suddenly answered.

"Jonas! Can you hear me?"

"Barely," Jonas replied in a loud voice. "Where are you? Is anything wrong?"

"No. We had to move some yearlings that were down by the river into the barn. They're dry now. Have you looked at the bridge?"

"About thirty minutes ago, Alexa and I crossed it. But water was already pouring over it."

"Well, it's impassable now. I just drove down there to have a look. I've never seen such a hell of a rain around here. I hope no one needs off the ranch anytime soon, 'cause that isn't going to happen for a while."

"Let's just hope to God we don't lose any cattle or horses in this," Jonas countered. "Call me if anything happens."

The two men exchanged a few more words and then ended the call. Jonas put the phone away and made himself go to bed. But even after his head was on the pillow and his body warm from the soft down covers, he felt very uneasy.

Was she dreaming? Pains were ripping through her back as masked nurses urged her to breathe deeply.

Your baby is coming, Miss Cantrell. Do as we tell you, and it will make your delivery much easier.

Baby? Delivery?

Panting, Alexa bolted straight up in the bed and looked around the darkened bedroom.

Oh God! She wasn't in the hospital. She'd been dreaming!

Just as that realization hit her, the pains in her back struck again, telling her that at least a part of her dream had been true.

Glancing toward the window, she noticed the rain was still falling, but not nearly as fiercely as it had been when she'd gone to bed. Her groggy gaze slipped to the small clock on the nightstand. Two-fourteen. She'd had enough sleep to feel rested, but something wasn't right. Had she pulled a muscle in her back?

She was swinging her legs over the bed to walk to the bathroom when another dull pain started in the middle of her back and radiated to the middle of her stomach.

Oh dear, the baby! Was this labor?

She visited the bathroom and then returned to bed, all the while waiting and hoping that her labor machine hadn't suddenly been set into motion. Yesterday, the doctor had assured her that there'd been no real signs of imminent delivery.

Stretching back out on the mattress, she

told herself not to get into a panic. The pains might be false and go away.

Her hopeful thinking was shattered in the next few minutes, as the pains grew more rapid and deep. Flood or not, the baby had decided to arrive. She had no choice but to wake Jonas.

Jonas had never been a heavy sleeper, and he heard Alexa's light footsteps long before she moved into his room.

"Jonas?" she called softly.

Already sitting on the side of the bed, he quickly switched on the lamp on the nightstand. "What's wrong, Alexa? Are you ill?"

"No, I—" Grabbing the lower part of her belly, she bent forward. "I think—the baby is—coming."

Leaping off the mattress, he grabbed her by the shoulders. "Alexa! Are you sure? It's not time, is it? I thought you had weeks to go!"

Catching her breath, she raised back up and looked at him. "The doctor said yesterday that the baby had already turned its head down. He said labor could happen anytime now. But his estimation was that I probably had another two weeks to go. Guess the little one has other ideas."

"God Almighty! Let's get you back to bed, and I'll call for an ambulance." He began to lead her out of his bedroom and toward hers.

Alexa groaned out loud, but her reaction wasn't from labor pains. "Jonas! You're not thinking! An ambulance couldn't cross the river now!"

She was right, Jonas thought wildly. Laramie had already informed him that the bridge was impassible. And no doubt, while they'd been asleep, the river had continued to rise. As a lawman trained to handle emergencies, he should have already thought that far ahead. But the idea of Alexa giving birth right here in the house, with no one but him for help, was far more rattling than facing a gun-toting maniac.

"Helicopter!" he exclaimed. "Surely they can get one of those in here."

"There's no place for it to land. Besides, the weather is still too rough out there. Oh God, what am I going to do, Jonas? The pains are—oh! Oh, no!"

She gave a loud gasp, and as she glanced down at herself, Jonas could see why. Amniotic fluid had dampened the front of her gown and was puddling on the tiled floor.

Without a word, Jonas swept her up in his

arms and carried her to her bed. After he'd fetched her a clean gown and helped her into it, he said.

"Okay. The water is high, but I'm calling emergency help, anyway. At the very least, a doctor can talk us through this," he said, trying to reassure both of them.

Back in his own bedroom, he tried his cell phone and found it to be totally useless. Apparently, the storm had knocked out the towers, making it impossible for signals to be sent.

Snapping it shut, he reached for the landline phone sitting on the nightstand and punched in 911 even before he got the receiver to his ear. The only thing he got in response was total silence, and he stared in horror at the useless instrument.

Surely this wasn't happening, he thought desperately. All the phones were dead. The bridge was impassable. Even with a large truck. That left him alone with Alexa. There were a handful of men staying in the bunkhouse. He could run down there and get one to help. But they were hardly doctors. They were all bachelors. They didn't know any more about childbirth than he did!

Hurrying back to her room, he sank onto

the edge of the bed and reached for her hand. She looked at him hopefully, and he suddenly felt like an incompetent failure.

"I hate to tell you this, Alexa, but the phones are dead. It looks like I'm going to have to deliver your baby on my own."

Her eyes widened just a fraction, but when she spoke there was no fear or panic in her voice. Jonas was amazed.

Her fingers squeezed his. "Well, you're the next best thing to a doctor," she said. "Ranchers like you are trained for this sort of birth, aren't you?"

Feeling helpless, he raked a hand through his rumpled hair. "Animals are hardly the same, Alexa!"

A grin crossed her lips, but the humorous expression suddenly disappeared as pain racked her body. "Same fundamentals," she finally managed to whisper. "You'll see."

"All right, honey." He brushed the hair back from her forehead. "Don't worry. We'll figure it out together. And I'll keep trying the phone."

Rising from the bed, he started toward the door.

"Where are you going?" she called out. "Not to boil water, I hope!"

The idea that she could joke at a time like this very nearly made him chuckle. But not quite. He was smart enough to know that a thousand things could go wrong when a woman gave birth to a child. If any of them happened with Alexa, if anything happened to her or the baby, he'd never forgive himself.

"I'm going to gather some things we might need. Rest as much as you can," he told her. "I'll be back."

A few minutes later he returned with several blankets, scissors, a wooden clothespin and a stainless-steel bowl with a clean cloth in the bottom.

"What's the clothespin for?" she asked between episodes of teeth-gritting agony.

"To clamp off the cord," he answered as he spread blankets beneath her to protect the bed. "I'm positive you'll want your baby's navel to look pretty, and since I don't have a clue how to tie it off, I'll just clamp it and let the doctor deal with it later. If and when we get across that blasted river," he added. "Now don't try to talk so much. Just concentrate on saving your energy."

As Jonas readied the rest of his things, he silently figured that it would be well past midmorning before the baby arrived. Perhaps even later. In the back of his mind, he vaguely remembered his mother talking about going through sixteen hours of labor with her first child, Jonas's older sister, Bethany. If that was the case, it would be a long wait before Alexa's baby arrived.

Jonas couldn't have been more wrong. He hardly had time to fill the stainless-steel bowl with water and sponge off Alexa's sweaty face before her pains increased to one right after another.

"I think you'd better look, Jonas! It's coming now!"

"That can't be right, Alexa. Less than thirty minutes have passed since you woke me!" He picked up his cell phone and punched 911 for the umpteenth time. The only sound in his ear was deafening silence.

Glancing down at Alexa, Jonas could see she was in agony. Her head was twisting back and forth against the pillow, and he wondered with amazement how she was dealing with the pain without any sort of help to ease it. She was being a rock, while his insides were gripped with fear at the idea of what was about to take place.

"I know…what I feel… Jonas! The baby's head…is there!"

Wanting to pacify her any way that he could, Jonas lifted the sheet and looked for himself. Excitement rushed through him as he saw the baby's head beginning to crown.

"You're right, Alexa! It's coming! Just hang on, honey. Push just a little, and let's see if we can get him here."

"I—am—pushing!" she gritted out.

"Okay, okay! Then try to breathe and relax. Maybe you're pushing too much."

She tried to do what he asked, but another pain struck hard. "Oh! Oh, Jonas!" She cried out loudly. "I'm—I'm splitting in—two!"

Reaching for his hand, she gripped it with all her might. Jonas was instantly amazed at the strength in her fingers, at the look of focused purpose on her face. She loved this child that was coming. Would always love it. Just like he would always love her.

Oh God, don't let me think about that now, he prayed.

"Come on! Just a bit more, sweetheart. The baby is almost here! Just one more push."

For one split second Alexa thought she was going to pass out from the pressure and the blinding pain, but then all of a sudden it was gone and she could hear Jonas exclaiming that the baby was out. A peace such as she'd never felt in her life settled over her.

Opening her eyes, she gazed down the bed to where he was still tending to her and the baby.

"What is it?" she asked groggily as she felt what little bit of strength she had draining out of her. "Is it okay?"

Before Jonas could reply, the baby let out a loud squall. The sound put a dreamy smile on her face.

"Your son sounds great," Jonas answered. "And he looks perfect. Let me finish here, and then you can see him."

Alexa somehow managed to rise up on her elbows to watch Jonas leaning over the bed, gently cleaning the baby's nose and mouth. The sight brought tears to her eyes, and she knew in that moment that no matter what the future held, she would be bonded to Jonas for the rest of her life.

Incredibly, once the baby was safely out and crying lustily, Jonas tried the cell phone again and was both amazed and relieved when the call went through.

After much confusion and numerous explanations to the emergency dispatcher, he was finally put through to the hospital, where a doctor came on the line to talk Jonas through the remaining things that needed to be done for mother and child. Jonas was grateful for the man's calm instructions, and before he hung up, he promised the doctor that he would bring the mother and newborn to the hospital as soon as possible.

Much later, after Jonas finished dealing with the last of Alexa's needs, he carefully placed the baby in her arms. The specialness of that moment, when she got her first close-up look at her son, was something that Jonas would never forget. So many emotions swelled inside him that he had to turn his back to her and move away from the bed.

"He's beautiful," Alexa murmured drowsily. "So beautiful."

Yes. He looks like you, Alexa. Beautiful. Precious.

Swallowing hard, Jonas turned back around to see she'd fallen asleep with the baby tucked safely to her side.

A few hours later Alexa woke to daylight streaming through the window. Jonas was stretched out beside her on the wide bed. He was sound asleep, his face lax and unguarded. Between them, nestled in the crook of her arm, her son was sleeping, too, and as she looked down at his sweet, tiny face, she felt a pang of deep longing and regret. How wonderful, how truly perfect, it would be if the three of them were a family. Jonas would love her baby. He would father it the way a child should be fathered, she realized.

But she was only dreaming a pleasant dream. Jonas had kissed her and held her. He'd even delivered her child. But he'd never once talked about love or forever. Would she be crazy to think he would ever talk about those things with her?

The question was still swirling around in her mind when she saw his eyes flutter open and slowly focus on her face.

She smiled and her heart swelled to such fullness that she could hardly breathe.

"Good morning," he said huskily. "Are you okay?"

"I'm—" She blinked as happy tears gathered in her eyes. "I'm wonderful. Thanks to you."

He propped his head up on one hand. "Don't give me the credit. You did all the work and then some. And I hope you don't mind me lying here next to you two. I wanted to stay close. In case you needed something."

Reaching across the baby, she touched his cheek. "I'll never forget what you've done for me and the baby. Never."

Sheepish color crept up his face, and he looked awkwardly away from her and down at the baby. "Don't make me out to be a hero, Alexa," he said lowly. "Hell, you have no idea how scared I was."

"Hmm. All I saw was a cool guy with a pair of steady hands." Seeing that her praise was embarrassing him, Alexa changed directions and pushed the thin blanket away from the baby's face. "Look at him, Jonas. He's the most precious thing. He has black hair like me."

Jonas smiled as he studied the baby's sleeping face. "Yes. I already noticed the hair."

"And look at his little fingernails. They already need to be clipped!"

"I described his fingernails to the doctor. He said that meant the baby was all ready to come out and greet the world. I'm relieved he wasn't premature."

She rubbed her thumb over the baby's tiny hand. "How much do you think he weighs?"

"About a half bucket of horse feed."

She chuckled. "Jonas, be serious! How much? Really."

"Oh, I'd say he's a pretty big boy. Maybe eight pounds or so."

A sigh parted her smile. "That will give him a good start."

A good start. Her life was just beginning, he thought enviously. While his felt as though it was ending.

Rising from the bed, he looked down at woman and child. If they belonged to him, if the three of them were a family, the whole world would seem like a bright and beautiful place. *For a while,* he thought sadly. And then, each time he was called away, he'd see disappointment in her eyes. Until finally that disappointment turned to downright disgust. He'd eventually lose her and the baby both.

No. Having this short time with Alexa now, knowing that she respected him as a simple cowboy, had to be enough.

"I'd better go fix us something for breakfast," he said in a voice husky with emotion. "Maybe in a little while the water will go down and we'll be able to drive to the hospital."

She reached for the cell phone on the nightstand. "And I'd better make a few calls to my family," she told him. "They're all in for a big surprise!"

* * *

By mid-afternoon, Jonas's projection turned out right, and with the baby carefully bundled in a car seat, he drove the two of them into Ruidoso, to Sierra General Hospital.

After a thorough examination of both mother and son, the doctor pronounced them both in excellent health and said there was no evident need for either of them to stay overnight in the facility.

Alexa happily declared that she felt as healthy as a horse, but she didn't argue when a nurse insisted that she had to be wheeled out of the hospital and wasn't allowed to walk.

Easing into the wheelchair, she told the attractive nurse, "This seems rather silly when I'm perfectly capable of walking."

The nurse smiled. "I'm sure in a few months' time, when your little guy starts crawling and walking, you'll be glad for the rest."

"I'll carry the baby," Jonas offered, extending his arms out to receive the child.

The nurse arched a suspicious brow at him. "Do you know how to handle a newborn?"

Laughing now, Alexa winked at Jonas. "I would think so. He delivered the baby."

"Oh," the nurse said. "Well, I guess you are qualified to act as Daddy. Congratulations."

"Congratulations is my line!"

The nurse was about to hand the baby over to Jonas when they all turned to see Quint striding quickly toward the group. A huge grin was on the man's face as he bent down and gave his sister a tight hug.

"You're something, sis!" Quint joked. "You had my little nephew in one of the biggest rainstorms we've ever had around here!"

Ignoring Quint, the nurse handed the child over to Jonas, who in turn pulled back the blanket so the other man could take a gander at his nephew. "I know you want to have a look at him. Would you like to carry him out to the truck?" Jonas asked, even though he was reluctant to hand the baby over.

Quint chuckled nervously. "Uh—you're doing just fine, partner. I might drop him. When he gets some teeth and a strong left hook, I'll try it. Right now I just want to see how much he looks like me."

"Sorry, Quint," Jonas told the other man. "He looks like Alexa."

Drawing closer to the two of them, Quint carefully studied the baby's face. "Damn, but

I believe you're right, Jonas! He even has my sister's big mouth."

"Quint!" Alexa scolded. "Just wait until you have babies! I'm going to insult every one of them!"

Quint threw back his head and laughed. "Okay, I'll be nice. So what are you going to name the little cowboy? Little Quint?"

Alexa rolled her eyes at her brother, then glanced shyly over at Jonas. "I'm going to call him Jonas David. If that's all right with Jonas."

Jonas felt as though someone had whammed him in the midsection. Naming the baby after him came as a complete shock. She'd never even hinted to him that she might do such a thing! What did it mean? Was she doing it out of gratitude? Because he'd delivered the child? Or was she trying to say, "I love you"?

Hell, hell, hell, Jonas. Get that word out of your system. Forget you ever heard it, because you're not ever going to hear it from Alexa.

"I—well, I'm surprised. And honored," he said.

Quint's brows shot up with surprise as he glanced from his sister over to Jonas. "Obviously the David is for our father. That was his first name."

"Yes," Alexa told Quint. "And I hope you weren't planning on using that name for one of your sons. But since you don't even have a girlfriend, it looks like that's not about to happen."

"Don't worry about me, sis. I'll catch up. When the time is right," Quint said coyly.

He gave Jonas a pointed look, while behind Alexa's wheelchair the tall, redheaded nurse cleared her throat.

"I hate to interrupt this family gathering," she said, "but I have to see Miss Cantrell safely to her vehicle before I can return to my post."

"Well, you go right ahead, Ms. Donovan," Quint told her. "I don't see anybody trying to stop you."

The nurse glared at him but said nothing as she pushed Alexa on out the revolving doors. The men followed closely behind, but once Alexa and the baby were safely ensconced inside the waiting truck, Jonas discreetly pulled Quint to one side.

"I've been needing to talk to you," Jonas muttered in a low voice, "but I haven't had a chance."

"I can imagine that. It's not every day a man goes around delivering babies." Smiling, Quint reached over and swatted Jonas affectionately on the shoulder. "If Alexa hasn't already thanked you, then I sure intend to. She's my darling little sister. I want her safe and happy. Always. Thank you for taking such good care of her."

"I'm glad that I was there for her."

Quint studied his face. "You don't look too happy about it."

Jonas let out a long breath. "I'm happy for Alexa and the baby. It's just that things are getting a bit—complicated."

"How do you mean?"

Jonas rubbed a hand over his face. Behind them, the nurse hurried back into the hospital. He said, "Your sister and I—we—"

"Look, Jonas, I'm not dumb," Quint interrupted. "She's named the baby after you. That tells me a whole lot."

Jonas shook his head. "I'm beginning to care about her, Quint. Really care. But you know why I'm here. You know that I'll be leaving when all this is over. I—I've been thinking about things, and I've decided I've got to tell her."

Quint glanced across the sidewalk to where

Alexa sat waiting in the truck. She was staring curiously out the window at the two men. As a result, he took Jonas by the shoulder and guided him a few steps farther behind the truck so that they'd be out of her sight.

"You're going to tell her that you're a Ranger?" Quint was shocked.

Jonas sighed. "I have no choice."

"But I thought that was something you didn't reveal about yourself."

Jonas looked down at his boots. "Normally, I don't. But Alexa isn't a part of this crime I'm investigating. And I trust her to keep my secret. I want to be honest with her, Quint. I want her to understand that my time here is limited."

Quint's features tightened. "So she won't get serious. Is that it?"

Jonas nodded.

"Is that the way you want it?"

"I don't have any choice in the matter," Jonas muttered roughly.

"Don't you?" Quint countered. "Being a Ranger doesn't mean you can't feel, love, marry."

Jonas's head jerked up, and he stared at the other man. "Believe me, Quint, your sister is a wonderful woman. She deserves more than me. I want her to know that."

"Do what you have to do, Jonas. Just make sure you don't hurt her. She lost Mitch. And then that handful of crap in Santa Fe just about crushed her. It's high time she had some joy in her life. When she told me she was naming the baby after you, I thought—well, I was hoping you might be the man who would finally be able to make her happy."

Suddenly feeling dead inside, Jonas shook his head. "You're looking at the wrong man."

Chapter Eight

The next day everything changed. Alexa's mother, Frankie, returned home from her trip to Texas. Along with her, friends and acquaintances began arriving on the ranch to bring gifts to the new arrival and express their congratulations.

His attention no longer needed, Jonas went back to work, and that afternoon he took the time to call Tyler Pickens. To his surprise, the man was receptive and even invited Jonas to meet him on horseback the next morning so that he could show him where the fence had been downed between the two properties.

As for Jonas's plan to talk with Alexa, he

was still waiting to find the right time. If there was such a thing.

Last night, after they'd returned from the hospital, she'd been so happy, he'd not wanted to spoil her first full day of being a new mother with such somber talk. And today, with the house full of people, he'd not been able to get any private time to speak with her.

Now another night had arrived, and several tasks on the ranch had kept him busy later than expected. As he left his office, he noticed the driveway was finally free of strange vehicles and the lights in the house had been reduced to a few dim glows. Apparently, the well-wishers had all departed, and the place had quieted down. But Jonas was smart enough to know that the house would never go back to being the personal quarters it had once been for the two of them.

And maybe that was for the best, he thought dully. Today, when he'd caught glimpses of the waves of well-wishers coming and going from the house, he'd been reminded that he was really an outsider and not a part of Alexa's life. For a while there, when the two of them had visited Alexa's grandfather, he'd almost forgotten that. But now he'd come to his senses, and as he entered the kitchen and climbed the stairs, he did so with the realization that his days near Alexa were nearing an end.

As soon as he stepped onto the staircase landing, he was instantly surprised to see Alexa's bedroom door ajar and a block of dim light slanting across the hallway. Would she be alone, or would her mother be up with her?

His heart beating faster than it should, he approached her door, paused and raised his hand to knock, but before he could rap his knuckles against the wooden panel, she called out to him.

"Jonas? Is that you?"

"Yes."

Stepping into the room, he instantly sensed that she was alone, and his gaze quickly fastened on her. She was sitting in a wooden rocker, the baby cradled to her breast. Her black hair flowed loosely around her shoulders, and in the glow of the lamplight it gleamed with a reddish tinge. He'd never seen anything more lovely.

"I didn't expect you to be awake," he said quietly. "But I'm glad you are."

Her eyes were soft as she smiled at him. "I'm glad I am, too." She glanced down at the baby. "J.D. was hungry, but he's had his supper and now he's sound asleep. Would you like to put him in his crib for me?"

Moving over to the rocker, he looked down at her and the baby and tried not to notice the way the neckline of her pink gown dipped between her breasts. Now that he'd seen her naked, he knew how beautiful she looked, and those memories made him long to kneel and touch her, slide his fingertips along her smooth skin.

"I would."

She shifted the sleeping baby so that Jonas could easily pick him up, and as he bent over Alexa to collect the child, he caught her flowery scent, felt her eyes gliding over the side of his face. For a split second he started to turn his head sideways and lean his face into hers. But if he kissed her, he wouldn't be able to think, to say what he needed to say. So he focused on the baby.

With the child cradled safely in his arms, he straightened to his full height and turned his attention to the slumbering infant. His thick black hair had been smoothed to one side, and his tiny fist was resting close to his mouth. The small cleft in his chin was exactly like Alexa's, and Jonas could easily imagine him as a boy galloping across the ranch yard on a spirited pony.

"Poor little thing," he murmured. "All those people coming in today, staring at him like a monkey in a zoo."

Alexa chuckled lowly. "Oh, Jonas, it wasn't that bad. None of them woke him. I doubt he even knew that anyone was around."

The baby felt so tiny, so vulnerable in Jonas's arms, and fierce protectiveness washed over him like the rain that had flooded the river. He didn't know why he kept getting such fatherly ideas about Alexa's child. It was foolish of him to think of her and little J.D. in such terms, but he couldn't seem to stop himself.

Two days ago, when the child had been born and he'd held him in his hands, Jonas had been shaken to the very core of his being. Helping bring a child into the world was a life-altering event for any man. But this was Alexa's child, and that made it all too special. And all too difficult to keep his heart hidden behind his Ranger's badge.

Deciding he'd held the baby long enough, he carried him over to the white wicker crib that had been placed at the side of Alexa's crib. After easing him into the cozy bed, Jonas carefully tucked the blue blanket around his shoulders, then lingered to make sure he was going to remain asleep.

"Mother is on top of the world," Alexa said. "I had to make her go to bed. Otherwise she was going to wear herself out."

He straightened away from the baby. "Frankie has a new grandson. She has reason to be excited."

"Quint is coming over tomorrow for another, longer visit with his nephew. I guess he's just a wee bit excited about the baby, too."

Jonas glanced at her. "Quint's coming over?"

"That's what he promised. But who knows if or when he'll tear himself away from the new ranch."

A few days ago Jonas had called Quint and told him about the incident with Tyler Pickens. Might be the man would want to join Jonas and the neighboring rancher on their ride to the fence line, he thought. But it was hardly necessary.

Suddenly she rose to her feet and closed the small space between them. Jonas couldn't help but notice how different she looked now that her stomach was flat and free from the mound of baby she'd been carrying.

"Have you eaten?" she asked.

He shook his head. "No. I'll find something in the kitchen later. I came on upstairs because I wanted to talk with you."

Her brows arched in a questioning manner. "You sound serious."

"I am." He let out a long breath. Then, reaching for her arm, he led her over to the bed.

A puzzled look puckered her features as she sat and then watched him walk over and quietly close the door. When he returned, he sank down next to her and reached for her hand.

After he folded her soft fingers inside his and rested their entwined hands on his knee, he said, "I really don't know how to do this, Alexa." His voice was strained and weary, and he wondered how one woman could make him so weak and vulnerable. "I've been thinking about it for days now. And I'm—well, I'm breaking the rules right now, but—" A heavy breath heaved from him. "I have to do this."

Confusion flickered in her blue eyes. "You're not making sense, Jonas."

A wry twist appeared on his lips. "No. I

expect not. And it's not going to make much sense to you even after I explain. But I—"

"What rules are you talking about? Surely you don't think you've behaved in an ungentlemanly way with me! That you have something to apologize for? We're—well, I like to think you and I are growing closer with each day. We are, aren't we?"

There was an anxious sort of hope in her voice, and the sound cut into him like a jagged knife inching its way toward his heart. "We are. And that's why I have to be honest with you, Alexa. I don't want you to get the wrong idea. About me—about why I'm here on the ranch."

Her gaze was questioning, searching as it raked back and forth across his face. "What does that mean? I thought you were here as the general manager of the Chaparral. Quint did officially hire you, didn't he? I mean, he must have. I've been writing out your paychecks right along with those of the other hands."

His face grim, Jonas nodded. "I was officially hired. And your brother has been a real stand-up guy to agree to all this."

Growing frustrated now, she leaned back slightly and frowned at him. "Jonas, whatever it is that you have to tell me, please just come out with it. It's not like I'm going to bop you over the head or anything."

Glancing away from her, he struggled to brace himself. "All right, Alexa, here it is. I'm more than the Chaparral's general manager. I'm actually a sergeant in the Texas Rangers. I'm here on assignment—an undercover assignment."

Jonas looked back at her just in time to see her shoulders sag, her eyes darken, as though he'd dealt her a heavy blow.

"You're not kidding. I can see that. But I— this doesn't seem real, Jonas." She paused and shook her head, as though she was trying to wake up from a dream. "And yet deep down it sometimes crossed my mind that you seemed more than just a rancher to me. Your clothing—the phone calls—some of the questions you asked."

Biting down on her lip, she looked away from him, and Jonas felt his heart fill with a heavy ache as an empty, almost defeated expression took hold of her face.

"Are you angry with me?" he asked gently. "For not telling you before now?"

Shaking her head, she thrust a trembling hand through her hair. "I suppose I should be furious. But strangely I'm not. How could I think of you as a deliberate conniver? Especially when you must have had good reasons not to tell me. You're a Texas Ranger! You guys are supposed to be honest and upright—the cream of the crop. You are, aren't you?"

At this moment Jonas didn't feel like cream, but more like scum. Normally, when he worked undercover, it didn't bother him to keep secrets. That was just a part of the job. But this time, he'd allowed himself to get too close to Alexa—to everyone on the Chaparral. Now they were all starting to feel like family, and that was not a wise place for him to be.

His fingers tightened around hers. "Other than your brother, who was first approached by my captain about this assignment, no one is supposed to know who or what I am. Quint agreed to the whole thing because the trouble I'm investigating might be happening right here on the ranch. I've not figured that out yet."

Alarm filled her blue eyes as they swung back to his face. "The trouble? What is it? What could be going on that's so awful the state of Texas sent you here?"

"Rustling. Stolen Corriente bulls and heifers are being shipped in from Mexico without papers or even their true owners being aware of it. The Mexican government doesn't want the cattle, the bulls especially, slipping into the United States. It jeopardizes the corner that their country has on the Corriente market. On the other hand, the United States doesn't want diseases crossing the border unchecked and spreading into our cattle market. As to why I'm here in this area of New Mexico, we got a tip a couple of months ago that this area was a stopping-off place for the rustlers. The drivers crossing the U.S.-Mexico border are probably routing the cattle through the New Mexico mountains, where they change hands and are eventually hauled to markets in Texas."

Alexa was in total disbelief. The idea of the crime seemed like something out of a Western movie, and the notion that some of the Chaparral's men might be involved in such a felony seemed even more incredible. But beyond all that was the realization that Jonas was not the man she'd believed him to be. As with her mother, with Barry, she'd not really seen the whole person, and that shook her more than anything.

"Surely you don't think some of our men

are in on this rustling business, do you? Have you seen any evidence of that since you've come here?"

He shook his head. "Not at all. In fact, as far as I can tell, nothing with the Chaparral men can even be remotely connected to the crime. That's why we contacted Quint to get me settled in a ranch and checking out the land. But I was having trouble latching on to any sort of lead. Until Tyler Pickens. Tomorrow he's going to show me where the fences were downed. I'm hoping something will come out of that."

Alarm prickled her skin. "So you're thinking the rustlers might have been in the back part of our property?" she asked. "God, Jonas, that's scary!"

His expression was sober, even a bit pained, and Alexa realized this whole thing must be putting him under an incredible amount of pressure. She didn't like the fact that she'd been kept in the dark by him and her brother, but throwing a tantrum about it now would be fruitless. The thing that was really tearing her apart was the knowledge that he'd come here without the intention of ever making the area his permanent home.

All this time, she'd been thinking, believing, he'd be here always. God, how wrong she'd been! Again!

"That's one of the reasons why I hated to tell you. You've just become a new mother. You don't need any added worries. But I— we—oh, hell, Alexa, I'm not saying any of this right. I've not done any of this the way I should have. I never should've kissed you— never should've showed you how much I want you," he muttered, with self-deprecation.

Like an injured dove, her heart fell. "Why? Because you always planned to leave?" she asked softly.

His head jerked as though her question had hit the mark.

Wiping a hand over his face, he looked away from her. "Yes. I suppose that's the simplest way to put it." He glanced back at her, and this time deep regret marred his face. "Alexa, I care for you very much. Surely you can see that, feel that, but I'm a Ranger. Deep down that's all I'll ever want to be. And it would be wrong for you to want more—expect more from me."

Pulling her hand from his, she rose to her feet and walked across the room. If she didn't put some sort of space between them, she feared she was going to quit breathing entirely.

She pushed the next word through a tight throat. "Why?"

Behind her, she could hear his heavy sigh, and then his hands were suddenly closing around the back of her shoulders, spreading their warmth straight to the center of her being. His touch affected her like nothing or no one ever had.

"Because I'm married to my job, Alexa. And I never know where that job might take me or how many hours I might have to spend away from home. When I was married to Celia, I was constantly being torn between my duty as a husband and a Ranger. I understood that she needed me and that she deserved my attention, but I couldn't always give her that. I failed her. And as a result, our marriage failed. Do you honestly think I would ever want to put you through that? I think too much of you to hurt you like that, Alexa."

She stared down at the floor and swallowed as aching emotions filled her throat. Maybe he was right. Maybe it would be impossible for the two of them to have a future together. Still, all she wanted to do was turn and fling her arms around him, to feel the warmth of his body, the hard circle of his arms holding her close.

"At least you're being honest with me now," she murmured. Then, biting back the tears that were burning her eyes, she turned and lifted her fingertips to his face. "And I—do understand how you feel. Really. But I think—"

She broke off as she suddenly decided to keep her words to herself. Tonight wasn't the time to argue a case for their future. He didn't know that she loved him. She'd only just realized it herself. She needed time to decide what her feelings meant for her future and that of her baby before she tried to convey them to Jonas.

"You think what?" he prompted.

She tried her best to smile, but it felt as though her face was cracking. "Nothing. Just that I'll talk to you more about this later."

"You're disappointed in me."

She shook her head. "How could I be? You're a good, honorable man."

Closing his eyes, he pinched the bridge of his nose with his thumb and forefinger. "Funny you should say that. I don't feel very honorable at the moment. To be honest, I feel pretty much like a heel."

"I don't know why," she said gently. "You never made me any promises."

He opened his eyes and gazed straight into hers. Alexa's heart thumped, then raced off at a frightening gallop.

"I didn't expect you to react this way. I expected you to be angry."

Angry? She was hurt, humiliated and shaken, she thought. Hurt by the knowledge that once his case was over, he could leave for Texas, without a backward glance. Humiliated at the fact that she'd fallen in love with a man who'd most likely never love her back. And shaken because she'd not been able to see all that from the very start. But angry? No. Being angry at Jonas for being honest with her would be even more foolish than falling in love with him.

"Jonas, I realize that you—the first day we met—that you thought I was a spoiled princess. That I considered only my own needs. But my parents didn't raise me that way, and I'm not that sort of woman. I'm stronger than you think, and I hope that before you leave the Chaparral, you'll eventually see that about me."

He reached up and touched her face, and her heart tumbled into a somersault of emotions.

"I'm beginning to see a lot of things, Alexa," he said softly.

For a split second, she thought he was going to bend his head and kiss her. She was so convinced that her breath caught in her throat, her lips parted in anticipation.

But either she'd thought wrong or he'd quickly changed his mind, and disappointment swamped her as he whispered a quick good-night, then turned and left the bedroom.

The next morning Jonas went down to the kitchen long before daylight and was surprised to find Alexa's mother, Frankie, working at the kitchen counter, while Reena was nowhere to be seen.

"Good morning, Jonas. Ready for a cup of coffee?"

"More than ready, ma'am. Thank you."

He headed to the cabinet to fetch a cup, but she waved him toward the table.

"Sit. I'll get it for you. That's the least I can do for you since you're going to have to suffer with my cooking this morning."

This woman, the matriarch of the ranch, had gotten up early to fix him breakfast, he thought, with dismay. He'd expected her to be the sort that would have Sassy serving her breakfast in bed. She certainly looked like the fragile, pampered sort. Like Alexa, she was a beautiful woman, especially for her age. And like Alexa, he'd misjudged her priorities.

"Where's Reena?" he asked as she handed him the coffee.

She was dressed in a pair of jeans and a plaid western shirt trimmed with piping, while her hair was brushed around her shoulders in a youthful style. She was totally the opposite of his own mother, who'd never cared about her looks or bothered to gussy up for her husband or anyone else.

"Her mother has a doctor's appointment early this morning, and Reena has to drive her. Mrs. Crow is ninety now. But the woman never learned to drive. She doesn't even like to get in vehicles, so Reena has to do a lot of cajoling to get her anywhere. Do you have grandparents, Jonas?"

"A paternal grandfather and a maternal grandmother," he answered. "The grandfather I see fairly often. The grandmother not so much. She moved to California to live near my mother."

She walked back over to the cabinet and dropped four slices of bread into the toaster. "Do you ever travel out there to visit?"

"I have. But it's been a long time. I'm not much on—" He caught himself just before he said, "Leaving Texas." "Traveling."

While he sipped his coffee, she filled two plates with bacon, eggs and toast and carried them over to the table.

"I hope you don't mind if I join you," she said as she eased down in the chair opposite him. "And please, whatever you do, don't tell Alexa that I ate bacon and eggs. She'd never quit scolding me." Smiling guiltily, she shook salt and pepper over her eggs, then handed the seasoning to him. "I'm not supposed to have them. My heart, you see. But a person has to have a treat once in a while."

For the next few minutes, she chatted about the ranch and how much she admired the way he was handling things.

"I'm just so relieved that you've come along and taken over things for Quint. Abe is— well, Abe. He's lovable but cantankerous, and Quint has always adored the man. But he's going to drive Quint to the grave if he doesn't let up on this ranch-building thing. And now the old codger has this wild idea to open up the old Golden Spur." She waved her fork at Jonas. "I'm thinking to myself that he must be getting dementia. Why else would he think there's gold still on the property?"

"Everybody has to have a dream. Abe is happy because he has many," Jonas said.

Frankie smiled at him. "That's a wise and very nice thing to say, Jonas."

It felt very strange to Jonas to be sitting at the table, sharing a meal with Alexa's mother. Since he'd taken the job at the Chaparral, he'd only spoken to her a few brief times. Yet she was treating him as though they were old acquaintances, and he could only wonder how it would be if things for him were different and how it might be if Frankie were his mother-in-law. But like Abe, Jonas was just nurturing a dream.

"Speaking of Quint, Mrs. Cantrell, I—"

"It's not Mrs. Cantrell, Jonas. It's Frankie. I'm Frankie to everyone," she interrupted.

"All right, Frankie. I was about to say that after you left for Texas, Quint wanted me to move into the house just in case Alexa needed someone. And—"

"And thank God that you did!" she said, ending his sentence. "Actually, I had talked that over with my son before I left. We both agreed that you should be in the house with Alexa. And now—well, just think how awful it would have been if you hadn't been around to help her. I hope you know how grateful she is—how grateful we all are for getting our little J.D. here safely."

"I didn't do that much. Really. But now that you're back home, I figure you won't be needing me. If you'd like, I can move my things back to the bunkhouse this evening."

She looked at him in horror. "Don't even think it! Now that Lewis is gone and Quint is staying on one of our other properties, it's a relief to have you in the house at night. I mean, it's not like we expect trouble way out here on the ranch, but women can never be too careful nowadays. Thugs might get it into their heads that we have cash or jewelry or other pawnable items in the house, which they'd like to steal. And with the bunkhouse nearly a quarter of a mile away, we can't count on the men hearing anything."

After Jonas had left Alexa's room last night, he'd been thinking that the best thing he could do for both of them would be to move back into the bunkhouse. He needed to put space between them and give them both time to breathe and look at things logically. But it looked as though he was going to have to forget that plan. There was no way he could go against Frankie Cantrell's wishes. What excuse could he give her that wouldn't sound lame? He couldn't tell her that he was falling for her daughter and was afraid that if he didn't turn tail and run, he was going to fall even harder.

"If that's the way you want it, Frankie, then I guess I'll stay put."

With a satisfied smile, she reached for a decorative thermos and refilled his coffee cup. "I'm glad. And I'm sure Alexa will be glad, too."

A few hours later, as Jonas rode one of his favorite horses toward Tyler Pickens's ranch, he tried not to dwell on his chat with Frankie or the warm way that Alexa's mother had treated him. Knowing that the woman thought he was someone other than who he really was bothered Jonas almost as much as it had bothered him to keep the truth from Alexa. But he couldn't allow his feelings to soften his resolve or undermine his training. Just because he liked someone or felt a pang of guilt didn't mean he could go around revealing his identity. He liked Laramie Jones, too. And it would be easy to confide in the other man. But if Jonas started crumbling in that way, he wouldn't remain a Ranger for long. He'd be kicked off the force or, at the very least, chained to a desk.

Even so, after Quint had informed him early this morning that he wouldn't be able to make the ride, Jonas had invited Laramie to join him. He valued the foreman's opinion, and though he couldn't tell him or Pickens about the rustling problem, he was hoping the three of them together could figure out what had taken place at the border fence. Could be that the downed wire had no connection to the case that Jonas was working on.

Later that afternoon at the ranch house, Alexa was caught up in taking care of little J.D.'s needs and receiving calls from well-wishers who were just getting the news about the baby's birth.

Laurel arrived just before supper time, and she took great pleasure in rocking the baby while Alexa changed into something suitable to wear to the dining table.

"This little guy of yours is just gorgeous!" Laurel exclaimed as she looked down at the baby cuddled in her arms. "He almost makes me forget what stinkers men can be. Please don't let this one grow up to be a self-centered jerk, Alexa."

Alexa laughed. "I can only control him up to a certain age, dear friend."

"Hmm. Guess you're right, so I'll just have to hope he has a kind heart. Like his mother." She looked over at Alexa. "So tell me, what was it like having Jonas deliver your baby? It had to be embarrassing. Was it?"

Easing down on the dressing bench, Alexa pulled a hairbrush through her long hair. "I didn't have time to be embarrassed," she admitted. "Besides, Jonas is—he made everything easy for me."

"I can hear something in your voice, Alexa. It's warm and soft and sounds suspiciously like love."

Alexa paused in her brushing as a painful lump filled her throat. Yes, she loved Jonas. It had snuck up on her and she couldn't stop it. But she wondered how much good that was going to do. He was a Texas Ranger. Oh God, the realization was still tilting the ground beneath her. All day today, she'd not been able to get anything he'd told her out of her mind. Sooner than later, he'd be leaving the ranch, going back to his home in Texas, to his prestigious job there. How could she live without him?

She sighed. "I—I suppose it is, Laurel."

"You don't sound any too happy about it. You still think Mr. Redman doesn't want a permanent relationship?"

Alexa didn't think it. She knew it. But she couldn't explain to Laurel, her mother or anyone else that Jonas was a Ranger, that he'd never planned to make his life here in New Mexico in the first place.

"He's made it very clear." Bending her head, she closed her eyes. "I don't know what's the matter with me, Laurel. I try to use my head and make sensible, logical choices, but my heart always seems to get in the way. Mitch was a great guy, but we both know he was wild and adventurous. I should never have fallen in love with him in the first place."

"But you were both very young, and you were a little wild and adventurous, too, at that time in your life. You didn't know the truck was going to crash or that he was going to be killed."

"I was very young then," Alexa admitted thoughtfully. "Not even out of my teens. But I can't use that excuse for Barry." She grimaced, with self-disgust. "I was so stupid, Laurel, for ever going to Santa Fe, for thinking I could ever live anywhere other than on the ranch and be truly happy, for thinking that a man like Barry was right for me. But I was bound and determined to move on from the accident, to change myself into something totally opposite from that young, foolish cowgirl. I didn't really love Barry. I tried to convince myself that I did. That I'd be happy with him. That was even more stupid of me. And now—"

"And now there's Jonas," Laurel finished for her. "And somehow I get the feeling that everything is different with this ranch manager."

Everything was different all right. When Jonas had kissed her so fervently at the springs, she'd taken every touch, every caress to heart. But now she could see that everything with him was temporary, even his desire for her.

"Tell me, Laurel, have you ever loved someone who didn't love you back?"

Groaning, Laurel tilted her face toward the ceiling. "Once. It was the most painful, humiliating thing I've ever been through." She leveled her gaze on Alexa. "But surely you're not thinking that your cowboy doesn't love you back. I just won't believe that for one minute."

"Laurel!" Alexa scolded. "You've not even met the man! You couldn't know something like that!"

She shook her head. "Alexa, I'm not blind. You're a walking vision. Most any man that you gave the chance to would fall for you like a brick. Now me—" she grimaced "—that's a whole other matter."

Laying the hairbrush aside, Alexa rose from the dressing bench. "Let's go down and see if supper is almost ready. Would you like to carry J.D.? Or shall I?"

"Oh, please, let me," her friend said. "It will probably be years before I have a child of my own. Tomorrow I'll have to settle for rocking a sullen tomcat." With the baby in her arms, Laurel rose from the rocker and joined Alexa at the bedroom door. "By the way," she asked coyly, "how did Jonas react when you told him you were naming the baby after him?"

"Humbly."

Totally unaware of the ache in Alexa's

heart, Laurel chuckled. "A humble Texan? This Jonas must be quite a man."

He was quite a man, Alexa silently agreed. He'd just never be her man.

Chapter Nine

Three days later, as dusk began to fall over the ranch yard, Alexa was sitting on the balcony of her bedroom, and just by chance, saw Jonas walk into his office.

This sighting of him was the first she'd had since he'd revealed to her that he was a Ranger. Since then he'd not returned to the ranch house until very late at night.

Yet each night she'd lain awake in bed, listening for his footsteps as he climbed the stairs, moved quietly past her door, then on to his bedroom. Each time she'd heard him, her heart had beat fast, her breath had caught in her throat and she'd hoped that he would come into her room, that he'd tell her he wanted her, that no matter who he was or what he was, he still wanted her. But her wishes hadn't come true, and now she was beginning to see that she was going to have to take matters into her own hands.

She'd lost Mitch. But losing him had been beyond her control. Her relationship with Barry had been too planned to ever be the real thing. Now, if she had any chance at all to make a life with Jonas, she had to take action. She couldn't mess up a third time.

After leaving J.D. in his grandmother's loving care, with the excuse that she was going for a walk, she headed outside. Straight to Jonas's office.

Inside the small room, Jonas had just taken a seat at his desk when his private cell phone rang. Seeing his captain's number, he answered it quickly.

"Jonas here."

"Can you talk?" Leo asked.

"Yeah. I'm alone. What's up? News from the border?"

Jonas was only one of many men who were working on this case. The Border Patrol, U.S. Customs, the Texas Department of Agriculture and even some county lawmen on the border were involved. Jonas had been placed in the middle, in hopes of catching the culprits en route.

"We're hearing that another load is expected to cross soon. But that could just be talk. Could be someone is just making noise down that way to throw us off."

"You think any of the undercover agents down there have been outed?"

"They don't think so. We'll see. I was hoping this thing would move in the next few days. If the rustlers are going to stop over in Lincoln County, you need to be there. But the Daniels trial is coming up next week. You're going to have to come back to testify."

Biting back a groan, Jonas massaged his taut forehead. "The Daniels trial! I thought that wasn't going to be coming up for several more months. Since when did the wheels of justice start spinning this quickly?"

"Since the prosecutor argued that the case should be put on the fast track. It's always best for the state to have fresh evidence. I don't have to tell you how the courtroom works—when months rock on, memories dim, and the horror of the thing fades. We want this monster behind bars, and you can help put him there. You have to be here, Jonas. There're no ifs or buts about it."

Leo was right. A good part of the San Antonio division had worked on the Daniels case for months. It had been a particularly horrific crime, with the accused beating and robbing an elderly farm couple of what few dollars they had in the house, then kidnapping their granddaughter from the same house with the intention of prostituting her in Mexico. Before the assailant had left the scene of the crime, he'd thought that setting the house on fire would cover his tracks. But thankfully, a neighbor had spotted the flames and called 911. A few weeks later, Jonas had caught up to the assailant and the girl in a small Texas border town.

"I'll be there," Jonas said in a clipped voice. "When?"

"The trial starts Wednesday. I'll try to get the prosecutor to narrow down the day that you'll have to testify, but that's always iffy. Anything could cause delays. I'll let you know Monday. In the meantime, keep up your work there."

After a few more words between the two men, Leo ended the call. Jonas slipped the phone back into his pocket and, with a weary sigh, leaned back in the leather chair. He'd never liked testifying. He didn't know of any man in his division that did like taking the witness stand, but it was a necessary evil of the job.

The idea of leaving this case for any length of time aggravated him. Particularly when he had the gut feeling that something was about to happen.

And you don't like the idea of leaving Alexa, either. You may as well admit that, Jonas.

Alexa. How he wished he could get the woman and her baby out of his mind. For the past few days, he'd deliberately tried to keep his distance. He'd told himself it was better that way. The more he saw her sweet smile, the more he looked at her and touched her, the more he wanted her.

Maybe it would be a good thing for him to have to go back to San Antonio, he thought grimly. Maybe time away from her and little J.D. would remind him that he had a life elsewhere.

Frustrated with his torn emotions, he pulled out the feeding schedule he'd been working on earlier and tried to concentrate, but he'd scribbled little more than three words when a light knock sounded on his door.

"Come in," he called.

The sight of Alexa stepping through the doorway was like a wham in the midsection, and without even realizing it, he rose to his feet and rounded the desk to greet her.

"Am I interrupting?" she asked.

"No. Nothing pressing."

The day had been hot, and she'd dressed accordingly in a pair of jeans and a blouse that exposed her arms and chest. Her black hair was swept into a ponytail, and he couldn't help but notice how tiny tendrils curled around her face.

He pulled out a chair and helped her into it. She smiled up at him.

"I'm not pregnant anymore, Jonas. You don't have to handle me like a flower."

To him, she would always be a flower, he realized. "Let me be the judge of that," he told her, then asked, "How's J.D.?"

Her smile deepened. "I swear, Jonas, I think he's grown since yesterday."

Facing her, he propped a hip on the desktop. Having her near made him ridiculously happy, filled him with a quiet joy that he'd never experienced before. The whole thing was scary.

"One of these days you'll look up and he'll be scampering down to the bunkhouse, crying to ride with the wranglers."

Her smile turned wry. "Yes. I've already thought of that. Sometimes when I'm holding him I just want to hang on tight and freeze every moment with him. Because I know that some day he'll be a man like you, and then I won't have any rein on him."

His heart winced. At least she had a child, he thought. He probably never would. "I wouldn't say that. Sons are usually always close to their mothers."

"Until they take a wife."

As soon as she said the word wife, Alexa could see an uncomfortable shadow cross his face. His reaction should have put her off, but she remained determined. She had to be.

For the first time in her life, a deep certainty had settled in her heart and assured her that Jonas was the man she wanted to spend the rest of her life with. This time she wasn't a young teenager dealing only with physical passion. This time she wasn't running from her past, trying to pretend she was experiencing real love. This time she knew exactly what she was feeling, and it was too special, too right not to fight for it—him.

"Aren't you a bit curious as to why I'm here?" she asked.

He shrugged. "I figured you were just out taking a stroll."

"I haven't seen you in three days. I wanted to find out why you've been avoiding me and the baby."

He grimaced; then glancing away from her, he released a long breath. "I've been very busy, Alexa. The fence thing with Pickens has given me fresh leads about the case."

"So you think that incident was caused by the rustlers?"

"Yes. When I looked over the area, it was easy to see that it was the perfect spot to load and unload cattle. There's a small boxed canyon nearby, where they can pen the cows long enough to let them have grass and water. There's also a mining road that leads past the canyon, across a corner of Pickens land, then to a county road."

"I'm not much on solving mysteries, Jonas, but it seems to me that these rustlers wouldn't have known about this secluded spot if someone who lives or works around here hadn't told them."

"Bingo," he replied.

"Dear God!" she exclaimed softly. "You haven't changed your mind about any of the Chaparral men being involved, have you?"

"No. I think it may be someone on the Pickens ranch. Certainly not Pickens himself, but one of his hands."

"How are you going to find him?"

"I can't infiltrate Pickens's men. And unfortunately, none of the Chaparral men are buddies with the Pickens men. I'll simply have to keep my eyes open."

There were many more questions she could have asked him about the rustling case, but she didn't. Sleuthing was his expertise, and she had every confidence he would handle the matter. She was here for far more personal reasons. Reasons that she didn't know quite how to express without sounding maudlin or clingy.

"Well, I'll be honest, Jonas. I've been thinking you haven't been around to see me because—well, because you don't want to."

A pinched look came over his features. "Alexa, I told you the reason that we can't have any sort of relationship."

Rising from her seat, she went to stand within inches of him. "You told me you were a Texas Ranger. Is that supposed to be an excuse for not loving, marrying, having children?"

She'd not meant to say any of those words to him, but now that she had, she was relieved they were out in the open. Maybe if she'd been more honest and open with herself these past years in Santa Fe, she wouldn't have made such mistakes with Barry. Maybe then she would have realized that leaving the ranch she'd always loved and pretending to enjoy a different lifestyle had not been the way to fill up the empty hole inside her.

He frowned. "I'm not giving you excuses. I'm giving you reasons. Sure, there are plenty of men in my division that are married. And they have good marriages. But it didn't work for me. Maybe I'm too selfish, too much like my father, to be a good husband. I don't know—I just know that you're too fine a woman and I—" His features suddenly softened as he touched his knuckles to her cheek. "I care about you too much to hurt you."

Her head shook back and forth as she tried to understand him. "That part about your father. What do you mean?"

Sighing, he stepped around her and walked over to the window. As he stared out at the falling twilight, he said, "I believe I told you that he was a police commissioner of a small town in Texas. Well, he was so devoted to his job that it put a constant strain on his marriage and himself. Yet he couldn't bring himself to let up. Then, during the latter years of his tenure, he struggled to run the department on a shoestring budget and with fewer than half the officers he needed. The stress ended up killing him. He suffered a major heart attack."

"You're not that obsessed, Jonas."

He looked over his shoulder at her. "Ask my ex-wife," he said starkly. "She'll be happy to tell you."

Alexa walked over to him and placed her hand on his arm. The feel of his warm muscle beneath her fingers was a gift, she realized. Just being near him was a gift.

"I'm thinking she didn't realize or understand the deep need you have to help other people, to right wrongs. I do know what it's like to serve the people."

His hazel eyes flickered with doubt, and she wondered if she was getting to him, if there was any hope that he could ever open his heart and his mind to a future with her.

He frowned. "She understood that I was

never there when she needed me. I was always focused on crimes and victims and justice."

Her fingers instinctively tightened on his arm. "That isn't a bad fault to have, Jonas."

"Oh? Are you telling me that you could put up with it?"

She sucked in a deep, bracing breath. "I'm not saying it would be easy for me. But compared to the faults that Barry, J.D.'s biological father has, it would be a pleasure to deal with this."

His interest piqued, he turned to face her. "You've not ever really told me about him. What happened between you?"

This time it was Alexa who was staring awkwardly at the floor. She wanted Jonas to know everything about her, yet that didn't take away the sting of enlightening him about her foolish behavior.

"I can't explain about Barry until I tell you about Mitch," she said lowly. She looked up at him, her eyes pleading for him to listen. Really listen.

"You did say you'd tell me about Mitch one day," Jonas reminded her.

Nodding, she said, "Looks like that time has come." Jamming her hands in the front pockets of her jeans, she moved away from him and began to walk aimlessly around the small room. "Mitch and I were both teenagers when we first met. He was a charming rascal and a wizard with a horse and a rope. When he came to work on the ranch, I fell in love with him from the very start, and for a long while, we were inseparable. Much to my parents' dismay. You see, Mitch was a hard worker and basically a good guy, but he had a wild, adventurous streak. A side that, unfortunately, often appeals to young, foolish females."

"Why didn't your father simply fire him? Send him on his way before you got deeply involved?"

"And break my heart? I would have found other ways to see him, and Daddy was wise enough to understand that."

"So what eventually happened?" he asked gently.

Pausing at the back of her chair, Alexa closed her eyes. "We'd gone to Ruidoso on Saturday night to party with friends. Some of us decided to drive out to the Hondo Valley, to a secluded spot where teenagers liked to gather. Mitch had had a few beers but nothing that would have impaired his driving, or so I thought. But on a sharp curve, he crashed the truck into a steep ravine. The impact killed him instantly and broke my leg, collarbone and wrist."

She opened her eyes to see him shaking his head in dismay. "God, it's a miracle you're alive today!"

"Yes. But back then, I couldn't see that part of the picture. I was devastated over losing Mitch. And I told myself I was never going to look at another cowboy. That I was going to get out of school and away from the ranch, find a new and different life. One that would make me happy."

"And did you?"

Grimacing, she walked toward him. "I went to college and got a degree in political science, and eventually, after working in the mayor's office, I got the job in Santa Fe. That's when I met Barry. We both worked in politics and shared the same sorts of goals, and I was very attracted to that part of him. And a man with tailored suits and shiny wingtips seemed far different and hardly a threat to my heart. He was a bit of a stuffed shirt, but he was a respectable lobbyist and a man I believed my parents would admire."

His brows arched with curiosity. "Did they?"

She tried to laugh, but the sound was garbled. "Not as a future son-in-law. They didn't think he fit me at all. But they were always polite with him, and neither of them ever tried to run my life. Barry visited the ranch once and was like a fish out of water. He hated it and I couldn't get him back to Santa Fe fast enough. I told myself that it was good he wasn't like Mitch. I never wanted my heart broken like that again."

His hazel eyes were solemn as they glided over her face in a long, searching sweep. "In other words, you didn't love the man."

"No. That's easy to see now. Back then, I suppose I was pretending. Trying to tell myself that I was creating the perfect life, where nothing bad would ever happen."

Jonas watched her bite down on her bottom lip and bend her head. His heart ached to take her into his arms, to press her close against his chest and never let her go. Her happiness was so important to him. And yet he could see that he was bringing misery to her life.

"What finally happened between you two?" he asked.

Her head lifted. "I told him about the coming baby. He pretended to be happy about it, but I could see he was disappointed. He had a lot of political plans, and I guess he was wondering how having a child out of wedlock would affect them."

"Didn't you want to be married?"

"Yes. But not right away. For some reason I couldn't explain, even to him, I wanted us to have more time together before we jumped into marriage. I suppose something deep inside must have been telling me that the relationship wasn't right. But then, about three days after I'd told him about the baby, I discovered, quite by accident, that he was involved in—let's just call them shady dealings with a couple of state senators. Nothing really illegal, or I would have turned him in. But edging toward unethical. When I confronted him, he merely laughed and told me to get used to it. That everyone who was anyone cheated to get to the top."

Jonas's teeth ground together as he wished his authority as a Ranger would allow him to cuff the man and throw him behind bars, where he belonged. "What a bastard!"

"I called him worse. But now—well, I'm just thankful he's agreed to remain out of our life."

She reached for his hand, and Jonas didn't

have the strength to keep his fingers from curving invitingly around hers.

"You see, Jonas, I've made some big mistakes. But I don't intend to make them with you."

As he looked down at her, everything inside him seemed to stop in stunned fascination. "What does that mean?" he asked.

She drew in a deep breath. "It means that I love you, Jonas. And I'm not going to let you simply walk away from me. Not without a fight."

She loved him? Oh God, he'd never wanted that from her.

Liar, just hearing her say the words has flung your heart over the moon. Admit it. Take her into your arms, and tell her you love her, too.

Fighting to ignore the voice inside him, Jonas slowly swung his head back and forth. "Oh, Alexa! You're confused. You're reading more into this thing between us than is really there. You're just feeling gratitude because I delivered the baby."

Leaning into him, she flattened her palms against the middle of his chest. Jonas wondered if she could feel his heart hammering, the heat coming from the blood throbbing through his veins. Being near her robbed him of his breath and his senses.

"Damn it, you know what I'm feeling. This!" he muttered.

Before he gave himself a moment to analyze his intentions, Jonas grabbed ahold of her shoulders and crushed her body close against his. Since the baby had been born, it was the first time he'd held her in such an intimate way, and he was wildly aware of her soft curves molding to the contours of his body and the fact that there was nothing between them but a thin barrier of fabric.

"Jonas, I—"

"Don't talk! For once, don't try to reason anything," he mumbled as his lips fastened over hers.

The raw, wild moan in her throat was like that of an animal calling to its mate, and the sound caused Jonas's hands to slip to her buttocks and drag the juncture of her hips directly against his manhood.

Her mouth fluttered open at the same time her fingers dug into the back of his neck. Somewhere inside him, he knew that kissing her was like playing with explosives. He knew the danger, but he couldn't resist or worry about the shattered pieces she might leave behind.

The kiss went on far longer than it should have, and by the time he finally managed to lift his head, Jonas realized he was breathing as though he'd been running. His insides trembled as everything shouted for him to kiss her again.

"You're not thinking at all, Alexa!" he said gruffly.

"Neither were you a few seconds ago!"

He groaned with misgivings. "You're right. I wasn't thinking and I—"

Before he could say more, she laid a finger softly against his lips. It was all Jonas could do to keep from kissing the soft little pad and sucking it into his mouth.

"Now it's time for you not to talk, Jonas. Just listen," she implored. "All I'm asking for is a chance. For you to consider a future with me and J.D."

"Have you forgotten that my home, my job, is in Texas?" he taunted. "Would you be willing to follow me there?"

"I would."

Her unwavering answer was like an unexpected tremor shaking the ground, scaring him, making it impossible to decide the best path to run to safety.

"Oh hell, Alexa. Don't you see? Don't you understand? That sort of blind devotion would never work! In no time at all, you'd be blaming me, resenting me for taking away the things you love."

"You're forgetting the fact that I love you."

Setting his jaw with firm resolution, Jonas stepped back from her and walked over to his desk. Staring unseeingly down at the feeding schedule, he announced, "I have to go back to San Antonio in the next few days. I don't know how long I'll be gone."

She hurried over to his side. "Why?"

"I have to testify at a criminal trial."

There was an almost frantic look to her face. "What about this case? And what are you going to tell the men? What will I tell Mother? She's grown fond of you, you know. And Gramps is already asking when you're going to come with me to show him his new great-grandson."

He swallowed as foreign emotions began to choke him. He'd never belonged to a close-knit family. His parents had merely tolerated each other in order to keep the family intact. His ex-in-laws had never been particularly warm to him, either. They'd blamed him for Celia's unhappiness, and he'd never been able to argue that point with them. But here on the Chaparral, he felt welcome, wanted, almost loved. To think of separating his life from Alexa and her family was very hard for him to do. But he would do it. Because in the end, he knew it would be best for all of them.

"Abe isn't going to drive over here to see the baby?" he asked.

"No. He hates driving. Actually, he hates leaving the ranch for any reason. I promised to bring J.D. over to see him in a few days. Would you be willing to go with me?"

She wasn't going to let up on him, Jonas thought. And deep down, did he really want her to?

Swallowing again, he said, "If I'm not called away. In the meantime, if I am called back to San Antonio, I'll have to tell the men that I have a sick mother or something back in my old hometown. I'll give Quint the real lowdown. But your mother and grandfather will have to hear the same story as the ranch hands. I'm sorry about that, Alexa. But that's the way it has to be."

Rising on her tiptoes, she pressed a kiss to

his cheek. "As long as I know you're coming back, that's all that matters."

Throughout the following week, Jonas returned to the house late in the evenings and left early in the mornings. Even so, he didn't ignore Alexa entirely, and she was thankful for that much.

A few times, he stopped by the bedroom and held J.D. for a while. Other times, he lingered in the kitchen long enough to share breakfast with her and her mother.

Alexa cherished the bits of his presence, and though she longed to spend time alone with him, she was grateful that he wasn't shutting her out completely. After their talk in the office, when she'd told him that she loved him, she did not bring up the subject again. Alexa didn't intend to.

He now knew how she felt. And she wanted him to take the time to really think about what that meant to him, what she and the baby meant to him. Maybe it would never mean anything to him. But right now her heart was riding on hope. That was all she had.

A full week and a half passed before Jonas finally received word from Leo to get back to Texas. Late that night, after spending the day riding along the old mining road at the back of the property, he climbed the stairs and knocked on Alexa's door.

She called out to him to enter, and he walked in to find her bent over J.D.'s crib, tucking a thin yellow blanket around the baby's shoulders.

"How is the growing boy?" he asked.

"Sleeping like an angel now," she said. Then, straightening to her full height, she walked over to him. "You look very tired, Jonas. Are you okay?"

He wasn't okay. He was exhausted from long hours in the saddle. He was also torn over the idea of leaving.

"I've been riding in the boxed canyon area all day. When I wasn't in the saddle, I was sitting out of view, watching. Nothing moved."

"I'm sorry."

He could see that she really was sorry, and her understanding was like a soothing balm on an angry wound. But Celia had been like that in the beginning. She had seemed genuinely interested in his work and had empathized when things had gone wrong or he'd come home exhausted after making little or no headway. If he was crazy enough to try to make things work with Alexa, how long would it be, he asked himself, before her interest turned to regret and resentment?

"I am, too. But that's not what I stopped by your room to tell you. My captain contacted me a bit earlier this evening. I have to leave in the morning."

He watched as disappointment filled her blue eyes.

"Oh. I'm going to miss you."

She was standing with her hands folded primly in front of her, as though she was reluctant to touch him or to say more. Her reticence bothered him. No matter what, he wanted the truth from her.

Groaning, he shook his head. "Hell, Alexa, don't you think I'm going to miss you, too?"

Shrugging, she moved toward him. "I honestly don't know, Jonas."

"Well, I will."

"Is that supposed to make me feel better about you going?"

"I can't change my orders," he snapped, then immediately sighed, with regret. "I'm sorry, Alexa. I don't even know why I'm bothering telling you this."

"I hope you're telling me because you think I deserve to hear it from you."

He did think she deserved that much from

him. That was exactly why he was telling her goodbye tonight, away from any would-be onlookers.

Bending his head, he stared at the toes of his boots. "I guess I do." His expression grim, he glanced up at her. "I also wanted to remind you that you're not to go anywhere near the boxed canyon while I'm gone."

"Why would I do that?"

He shrugged. "You mentioned that you planned to start riding again soon. I just wanted to remind you not to go in that direction. We have no idea when or where the rustlers might strike again. I don't want you caught up in something that could be extremely dangerous."

"I'm going to the doctor for my month's checkup next week. If he tells me it's okay for me to ride, I promise I'll not go in the direction of the canyon. In fact, I'm so out of shape from the pregnancy, I wouldn't be able to ride that far, anyway."

He visibly relaxed. "Good. I mean, I'm glad that you understand the seriousness."

"I do. So who's going to be giving orders to the men? Is Quint going to come home and run things while you're gone?"

"Not unless it's necessary. Right now he's

planning to stop by every other day and make sure things are going okay. While I'm away, I think he's going to give Laramie partial reins."

It was a warm night, and beyond the open door to the balcony, Jonas could see a sliver of a moon hanging just above the mountaintop. Other than the faint ticking of a clock, the bedroom was quiet. The lights were dim. All the while he'd been standing in front of Alexa, talking as though he had good sense, part of him had been screaming to pick her up in his arms, to carry her to the bed and make love to her.

But he knew enough about women to know that she hadn't recuperated enough from childbirth to be ready for lovemaking. Which was probably for the best. If he ever was stupid enough to make love to her, he'd be a lost man.

She swallowed, then said, "I suppose that once your case is solved, Quint will have to hire someone permanently to take your place."

"Yes. I understand he's planning to move into the ranch house he's been renovating. But that's down the road, Alexa." And he didn't want to think about the day that he'd be going away for good. "Right now I'd better go get my things ready to leave in the morning."

"Will you be eating breakfast?"

"No. Tell your mother goodbye for me."

"I will."

She stepped closer, and he shivered inwardly as she curled her arms around his neck.

"I want you to remember me—this—while you're gone," she whispered.

Her lips were suddenly on his, and Jonas was assaulted by a flood of sweet sensations as the kiss deepened, then softened, then finally ended completely.

Breathing in deeply, Jonas rested his forehead against hers. "We'll talk about this—you and me—when I get back," he murmured.

She leaned her head back enough to look into his eyes. "No. We're all talked out, Jonas. We both know that. When you get back, we're going to do more than talk. We're going to make love. Think about that while you're in Texas."

Chapter Ten

A week after Jonas arrived back in San Antonio, the Daniels trial was in full swing, and he, along with a fellow Ranger, appeared at the Bexar County Courthouse to take the witness stand.

After two days of sitting on a bench outside the courtroom, neither man had yet been called to testify, and Jonas was finding it difficult to hide his annoyance.

"I don't know about you, Wes, but I've had a belly full of this," he said as he paced back and forth in front of his friend and coworker. "Don't these prosecutors know our time is precious?"

The other man tossed him a droll smile. "Our time is the least of their concern, Jonas. Just sit back down and relax. Try to get your mind on something else."

Hell, Jonas *had* his mind on something else, he could have told the other Ranger. That was the problem. Instead of concentrating on the facts of the Daniels case, he was thinking about the Chaparral and the canyon and wondering if the rustlers had hit the area while he'd been away. But he was thinking about much more than that: his mind was fastened on Alexa and her baby son.

Once Jonas had returned to his home here in Texas, he'd hoped that everything would go back to normal. He'd hoped that the deep connection he felt to Alexa would fade, and he'd be able to put her and the baby in proper perspective in his life. Instead, he couldn't stop imagining the three of them as a family unit. Or Alexa's promise to make love to him when he returned to the Chaparral.

Miserable with his churning thoughts, Jonas forced himself to sink back down on the wooden bench, beside his partner. He was just crossing his ankles out in front of him, preparing for another excruciating wait, when he caught the sound of a swishing door and then of a pair of high heels clicking on polished tile. At the same moment Wesley's elbow nudged his side.

Turning his head toward the opposite end of the corridor, he spotted the assistant DA striding quickly toward them. It was Madison Taylor, a tall blonde who'd worked in the DA's office for several years. Jonas had become acquainted with her when she'd been just a lowly public defender, and after his divorce from Celia, he'd dated her a couple of times. But there had been no chemistry between the two of them, and he'd mainly gone out with the woman because she'd been the one doing the inviting and he'd not wanted to appear snobby. Thankfully, she'd recognized there was no romantic spark between them, and they'd agreed to remain friends.

As she grew nearer, both Jonas and Wesley rose to their feet, but she quickly shook her head.

"Relax, boys. I only came out to tell you that the remainder of the afternoon is going to be taken up with arguments over admissible evidence. You two are dismissed until tomorrow morning at eleven, when court reconvenes."

"Damn it all!" Jonas fumed.

"I'm outta here," Wesley said quickly. "I'll see you in the morning, Jonas."

As the other Ranger made a quick getaway to the elevator, the assistant DA cast Jonas an apologetic look. "Sorry, Jonas. I know you're tired of waiting. But sometimes these things move slowly."

The woman standing before him was dressed in a professional, yet very feminine, red suit. Her natural blond hair was smoothed into an attractive pleat, and her features were pleasing to the eye. Yet when he looked at her, he felt none of the things he felt when he gazed at Alexa. What did that tell him? That he was half-dead or in love?

He heaved out a heavy breath. "I'm on a case, Madison."

"You're always on a case." She opened the cell phone she was carrying and began to check her messages.

"That's right," he said sharply. "You prosecutors would be out of a job if it weren't for us lawmen rounding up the criminals for you. And we sure as hell can't round them up while we're sitting in a courthouse, waiting for some judge to decide if he wants to get the ball rolling or listen to a bunch of lawyers argue."

In spite of Jonas's tirade, she continued to scan the phone in an unconcerned way. "That's our job. We get paid to argue." She glanced up at him. "You look like hell, Jonas."

He felt like it, too. "Thanks. Maybe I'll pull some sympathy from the jury."

She snapped the phone shut. "I haven't seen you around in a while. Everything going okay?"

If this woman had asked him the same question two months ago, he would have given her a ready yes and meant it. Back then he'd focused on nothing but his work and his little ranch, everything had been going smoothly and he'd been happy. Or had he? God, he didn't know anymore. How was it that Alexa made him happy and sad at the same time? How could one woman and a tiny little boy have him so mixed up?

"Yeah. Sure, Madison. Everything is fine. Thanks for asking."

He assured the DA that he'd be back tomorrow, then quickly left the busy courthouse. As he made his way to his parked truck, he fought the urge to pull out his cell phone and punch in the Chaparral's number.

He desperately wanted to hear Alexa's voice, to assure himself that she was okay.

But he wasn't going to give in to the urge and call her. He couldn't distance his heart from her that way, he argued with himself.

When you get back, we're going to make love.

Her whispered promise had continued to haunt him, and he wondered if he was fighting a losing battle. Maybe making love to Alexa was the answer to everything. So far they'd only shared a few heated kisses. Having sex might show both of them that they weren't compatible at all. Then everything would be fixed.

Everything except his heart.

The next evening, Alexa arrived at Apache Wells to show her grandfather his new great-grandson for the first time. Abe, who'd always been an iron man in front of his granddaughter, was reduced to tears when she placed the baby in his arms.

"Now here's a real little cowboy!" He wiped his watery eyes on the sleeve of his shirt before he settled himself and the baby in a willow rocker out on the front porch. "Just look at these hands, honey. He's gonna be big, big enough to knock a man's tooth out if he has to."

"Gramps!" Alexa scolded. "J.D. isn't going to be a fighter."

"Who says? He sure as hell ain't gonna be a little wimp. I'll see to that! I may be old, but I'll be around long enough to see that you raise this boy right!"

Smiling down at the two of them, Alexa said, "I plan on you being around for a long time, too, Gramps." She bent down and kissed his creased cheek. "Will you two be all right while I go in and make us something to eat?"

"Don't worry about me, honey. I know all about babies. Just delivered a stud colt day before yesterday. After we eat, we'll take little J.D. down to the barn and show him."

Alexa went inside and headed to her grandfather's cluttered kitchen, all the while thinking she wasn't about to tell the old man that J.D. was still too young to see much more than shapes that were very close to his face. It made her happy to see Abe enjoying the baby, and she wasn't about to spoil his fun.

My job is in Texas. Would you be willing to follow me there?

Jonas's question pushed at the fringes of Alexa's thoughts as she rummaged through the refrigerator. She'd answered him honestly.

Yet she knew that leaving her home, her family, behind would not be easy. Abe was getting older. He couldn't have too many more years to spend on this earth, and she wanted him to have time with his great-grandchild. Her mother's health was much better now, but Alexa knew that could change if someone wasn't near to make sure she took care of herself.

Yes, it would be perfect if Jonas wasn't a Ranger, if he was simply a cowboy and a ranch manager. *Dear God, how ironic that idea was,* she thought wryly. After years of swearing off cowboys, she was now wishing the man she loved was nothing but that. She was envisioning a perfect world, and as far as she'd learned, nothing about holding a family together was perfect. Or easy.

If Jonas ever decided that he loved her, if he could bring himself to want her and the baby permanently in his life, then she would gladly make her home in Texas with him. After all, she wasn't a poor woman. She could afford to fly back for visits as much as she wanted.

Yes, living in Texas could be worked out, she decided. The real problem was getting Jonas to realize the three of them belonged together.

* * *

On a Friday, at the end of the second week after Jonas had returned to San Antonio, he was finally called to the witness stand. The prosecution's questions were brief and to the point, and his hopes began to lift. If the cross examination was just as short, he'd be out of the courtroom in no time and back on the road to New Mexico before the day was out.

Unfortunately, it didn't turn out so smoothly. When his answers included forensic evidence, the defense immediately called for a delay. Arguments between the state and Daniels's attorney swiftly ensued, and a big uproar erupted over evidence made available to the defense.

Fed up with the whole thing, Jonas went to his captain and tried to argue that Wesley could tell the court everything that needed to be said. He tried to convince Leo that he was needed much more on the rustlers case than in the Bexar County courtroom. But Leo wouldn't budge.

Three long weeks passed before Jonas was finally able to finish up his testimony and get cleared by his captain to leave San Antonio. He immediately chartered a small plane to fly him straight to the Ruidoso airport, and once there he called Laramie to come fetch him.

Now, as the two men drove up the pine-lined lane toward the ranch, twilight was falling, casting the graveled road into deep shadow.

"I hope your mother is doing better now," the other man said as he steered the truck past the house and on toward the ranch yard. "I take it that she is. Otherwise, you wouldn't be back."

If the trial could be compared to a sick mother, then all was well, Jonas thought. Only minutes ago he'd gotten a text message from Leo. The jury had turned in a guilty verdict after a little more than an hour of deliberation. In spite of all their delays, the defense had not been able to camouflage the truth to the jurors. And in the end, Jonas realized, he'd done his job. He had to feel good about that. No matter how much he'd missed Alexa.

"Yes, she's better. And it's good to be back. Has Quint been keeping in touch?"

"Calls me every day. But we've not had any problems to speak of. One of the men broke his finger fixing a truck flat. And I'm still having trouble finding all the alfalfa we need, but that's not unusual. I'll find some, if I have to go all the way to Idaho to get it."

"What about the fence with Pickens? Anything else like that happen?" Jonas asked as casually as he could.

"Nope. I had a couple of the hands ride the whole border fence just last week. They reported that all was fine."

Jonas didn't know whether to be relieved or disappointed at that news. He wanted to catch the rustlers, but it puzzled him that they'd not returned while he'd been away dealing with the Daniels trial. It made him wonder if information had been leaked somewhere. Could be that Pickens had become suspicious himself over the incident and had made some remarks to his hands, and these remarks in turn had eventually made their way to the rustlers.

But Jonas wasn't going to worry about the case tonight. He was going to see Alexa and the baby. Right or wrong, that was all he was thinking about.

Laramie parked the truck in its regular spot near one of the cattle barns, and after a bit more conversation, he bade Jonas good-night and left for the bunkhouse.

Jonas headed straight to the house, and as he neared the low stone wall that bordered the backyard, he spotted Alexa sitting on the patio, flipping through a magazine. She was wearing a sundress with bright red and yellow flowers, and her feet were bare.

Seeing her again filled his heart, and these emotions that swelled his chest and thickened his throat. And he realized that he could no longer deny that he loved this woman.

For three long weeks, he'd tried to forget her, tried to tell himself that he didn't want her. None of it had worked, and now he couldn't stop himself from hurrying straight to her side.

His footfalls must have alerted her, because she suddenly looked up and spotted him crossing the yard. With a little cry, she flung the magazine aside and leaped from the chair.

"Jonas! Oh, Jonas!"

The next thing he knew, her arms were around his neck, and as their lips met, nothing else mattered. Touching her, kissing her, was like coming home. The cold emptiness he'd been feeling for the past weeks was swept away with her heated welcome, and he didn't bother to wonder who might be watching them.

"Alexa," he finally mouthed against her lips. "This is… I've been thinking about you—this—for so long! I've missed you."

"And I've missed you."

To underscore her words, she planted her lips on his, and for the next few moments, they were too caught up in the heated contact to say another word. She felt so good in his arms. So right. At this moment he felt as if he could hold her forever and die a happy man.

Eventually, though, Jonas forced himself to lift his head before he lost all control. "Where is everyone—the baby?"

Twisting her head, Alexa looked behind her, under the eaves of the patio. "J.D. is over there. Asleep in his bassinet. Sassy is out for the evening, and Mother has gone on an overnight shopping trip with a friend."

"You're here all alone?"

She chuckled sexily. "I know you probably don't like the idea of me being alone and unprotected, but it's perfect timing, don't you think?" Grabbing his hand, she pulled him toward the baby. "Let's get J.D. and go upstairs," she whispered urgently.

Jonas opened his mouth to tell her that they needed to slow down, to argue that it wasn't time for them to make love. That maybe it would never be time. But his mouth refused to work.

These past days without her had left him

empty and hungry. He wanted her, and she wanted him. He was tired of fighting the logic of that reasoning.

She placed the baby in his arms, and together they entered the quiet house and climbed the stairs to her bedroom. Inside the dimly lit room, he placed J.D. in his crib. Then, after making sure the baby was comfortably settled, he turned to reach for her.

"This is insane, Alexa!" he mouthed against her lips even as he felt her fingers reaching for the buttons on his shirt. "I've not been here five minutes!"

"You've been gone a long time, Jonas. Too long," she said as she smothered his face with kisses. "I want every moment I can get with you!"

She pushed the shirt off his shoulders, and he groaned as her head tilted forward and her lips glided against the heated skin of his chest.

"You—you've had a baby and—"

Lifting her head, she smiled as though she understood the awkward question he was trying to ask. "Nearly two months ago. And my doctor put me back on birth control that's good for breast-feeding. You don't need to worry about anything."

Jonas should have been worried about a thousand things, but he pushed them out of his mind as he brought his hands up to her hair and threaded his fingers through the shiny black waves.

"Are you sure you want this, Alexa? I mean, really sure?"

She nuzzled her cheek against his. "If you thought that my being away from you for three long weeks was going to change my mind about you—us—you're wrong. I know what I want."

Jonas knew what he wanted, too. And with her already standing in the circle of his arms, there was no way he could deny either of them.

Wrapping her tightly in his arms, he kissed her until Alexa was certain her knees were going to buckle. Then, finally, he lifted his head, and as they both gulped for air, he went to work easing the straps of her dress down over her shoulders.

As the smooth fabric slid down her body and pooled at her feet, she shivered with longing and, with her breath in her throat, waited for him to react. Because she'd been feeding J.D. only minutes before he'd arrived, she wasn't wearing a bra, and now his eyes feasted on her breasts, the brown areolae and moist nipples. His hot gaze thrilled her long before his hands touched her, and she moaned deep in her throat as he dragged her against him, brushed his bared chest against the sensitive nubs, while his mouth sought the tender curve of her neck.

Every nerve, every muscle in her body began to hum with heat and excitement as his lips began to explore first her neck, her shoulders, then, finally, the smooth, plump curve of each breast.

She reached for the waistband of his jeans and worked loose the button. As her fingers eased down the zipper, she could hear his sharp intake of breath and knew that he was feeling the same urgency she felt that he needed her, wanted her, and this time he wasn't trying to hide anything.

"Make love to me, Jonas," she whispered desperately. "Don't make me keep waiting."

Her plea had him lifting her into his arms and carrying her to the bed. After he'd laid her down on the smooth bedcover, he hurriedly removed the remainder of his clothes, then joined her on the bed.

Across the room, the door to the balcony stood open, and the night breeze wafted across their bodies like a caressing hand. She started to ask him if the air was too cool for him, but she quickly decided the question would sound insane. As he pulled her into his arms, she realized that both of their bodies were so hot to the touch, they felt as though they'd been dangled over a fire and were now on the verge of combustion.

"I've thought of this for so long, Alexa," he murmured as he pressed kisses along her cheek and across her chin. "And while I was gone, I kept imagining you like this. It was hell thinking about you and not being able to touch you."

His words soared through her heart like a high-flying bird. "I wasn't sure, Jonas. I wasn't sure that you would ever want me like this." Her hands cupped his face as she looked into his eyes. "But now—do you know what it does to me to touch you like this? To have you lying next to me?"

"Oh, baby," he said, with a soft growl. "Let me show you what it does to me."

He eased her back against the mattress, and Alexa closed her eyes and let the magic of his mouth and hands swirl around her, lift her to a warm, sweet place where there was nothing but him. Him loving her.

Soon, though, the warm, delicious sensations pouring through her became too much to bear, and it was all she could do to keep from crying out as she thrust her fingers into his sandy-brown hair and twisted her body back and forth beneath his as she sought the relief that only he could give.

Partial ease finally arrived when he split her thighs with his knee and entered her with one deep thrust.

The intimate connection momentarily stunned her, and for a second, all she could do was cling to his shoulders and pant for breath. Then just as quickly, wild, sweet exhilaration shot through her veins, sending heat and need rifling through her like a speeding bullet.

Groaning, she wrapped her legs around him and arched her hips toward his. After that, all sense of control seemed to leave her body. Suddenly and completely, she became his, and she could do nothing to stop the exquisite journey he was taking her on.

She lost all sense of time, of the long, long minutes ticking away, until she became aware of sweat slicking their bodies, of his harsh breaths above her and the sound of her heart hammering wildly in her ears. But it was the pounding thrusts of his body that were snatching her breath and pushing her ever closer to the edge of the cloud on which they were riding.

A choked noise sounded in her throat as she tried to bite back a cry of utter pleasure, while above her Jonas could feel her body tighten and arch into his.

Certain he was going to float away, he allowed his hands to dive urgently beneath her hips, and he clutched her tightly to him as he cried her name and felt himself pouring into her.

Eventually, after her breathing had returned to normal and she was lying alongside Jonas, Alexa realized one incredible thing. Until tonight, until Jonas, she'd never made love.

Nothing could compare to what she'd felt with this man who was now stroking her hair and kissing her forehead. Love and desire had twined together like the braid of a lariat, and the bands had wrapped tightly around her heart, squeezed it with bittersweet pleasure, even while his body had driven her to shaky heights.

Her movements languid, she reached for his hand, and he drew her fingers to his lips.

"I didn't know I could want like that," he

whispered hoarsely. "I didn't know it would be like this between us."

Tears stung her eyes as she tried to speak, tried to push her words through a throat thick with emotion. She wanted to remind him how much she loved him. She wanted to tell him that he was holding her heart in his hands. But she held it all back, afraid to ruin these precious moments of being in his arms.

"Neither did I," she murmured.

He nuzzled his lips against her neck, and with a satisfied groan, she turned to face him.

"It's gotten dark outside," she said as she rested her palms against his chest. "Are you hungry?"

A chuckle stirred his chest. "I am," he said huskily. "But I don't want either of us to move. Not just yet."

Just as lips moved to cover hers once again, a faint whimper sounded from J.D.'s crib.

Jonas lifted his head to listen. "Is he waking?" he whispered.

"Probably. We'll know in the next minute or two."

Deciding to make use of the time, Jonas bent his head to kiss her again. But his mouth only managed to make contact before the baby cried loud enough to say he didn't want to be ignored.

"He shouldn't be hungry," Alexa said. "I'll see if I can figure out what he wants."

She started to rise from the bed, but Jonas put a hand on her shoulder. "Let me," he insisted.

After pulling on his boxer shorts, Jonas switched on the lamp and bent over the crib.

"What's the matter, little guy?" Jonas crooned to the baby. "You want to get up and look around?"

Carefully, he lifted the swaddled baby up from the crib and into his arms. J.D. quieted instantly, and Jonas carried the infant over to a nearby window, where faint shafts of moonlight streamed through the glass panes and illuminated the child's face.

"He's grown a lot since I've been gone," he said to Alexa. Then, bending his head, he kissed the child's forehead and breathed in his soft baby scent. J.D. gurgled at him.

Alexa's soft chuckles sounded behind him at the same time that her arms slipped around his waist and her hands flattened against his midsection. The sound of her laughter, the feel of her body next to his were surely as good as a piece of heaven, he decided.

"You're so good with him, Jonas." She rested her cheek against his spine. "Did you ever want children?"

"Sure I did," he said lowly. "When Celia and I first married. We had it all planned. The kids, the ranch, even down to the cattle and horses we'd raise." He heaved out a heavy breath. "I have the ranch now. And a small herd of cattle and a handful of horses. I don't have the wife or kids. But I have no one to blame but myself for that."

She moved from around his back, and resting her cheek against the side of his arm, she glanced up at him. "Really, Jonas? Somehow I don't believe you should be shouldering all the blame."

Looking away from her sweet face, he lifted a finger to the baby's black hair and began to smooth it gently to one side.

"You should believe it," he said gruffly. "Because it's true."

"Have you ever stopped to think that Celia might have been too needy? That she didn't understand or appreciate your job or the sacrifices it would require both of you to make?"

He stifled a groan. "She wasn't a bad person, Alexa. She tried. And I didn't."

She grimaced. "I don't believe that, either.

Or—" She continued to study his face. "Did you decide you didn't really want to be married to her?"

If there was a guilty look on his face, he wasn't going to try to hide it from Alexa. She needed to see the man he really was. And maybe then she'd come to her senses and decide she didn't love him.

Is that what you really want, Jonas? Do you want her love to turn to disrespect? Do you want her to turn her back on you once and for all?

The questions made his insides shudder with a black fear that he'd never faced before. More than anything he didn't want to make a mess with Alexa's life. He didn't want to hurt her as he'd hurt Celia. But to think of life without her was like looking into an empty hole where even his own echo couldn't be heard.

"I wanted to be Celia's husband for a while," he admitted bleakly. "But then it seemed that the more I tried to please her, the more demanding she got. The more I tried to give of myself, the more needy and clingy she became. I was probably the reason for that—I don't know anymore. I just know that I was suddenly seeing the same

woman that my mother had been with my
father. And I didn't want to live through that
sort of hell—the same hell that my dad had
gone through." He drew in a breath, then released it in a weary sigh. "So after a while
I suppose I subconsciously started to draw
away from Celia. Both physically and emo-
tionally."

Her hand moved up and down his arm in a
soothing gesture. "You've never told me much
about your family," she said. "Especially your
mother. Are you not close to her?"

"Not very. She's a stern sort of woman. I
can't hardly recall a time that she hugged or
kissed me or my siblings. I'm sure she loves
me and my brother and sister—in her own
way. But while we were growing up, she was
always more concerned about keeping the
household running and money in the bank.
She hated Dad being a lawman. All the years
they were married, she hounded and whined
and nagged for him to quit the job and be
something else. Mom was all about business
instead of emotions. She didn't have a clue
that Dad was unable to be something else. A
lawman was who he was, what he was. The
job might have killed him, but at least he died
doing what he'd chosen to do." He looked at

her and was suddenly embarrassed as a sheen of moisture glazed his eyes. "Is that too much for a man to ask?"

Her gentle smile went straight to his heart.

"Put the baby back to bed, Jonas," she whispered. "We're not going to talk about this anymore tonight. We're going to forget about yesterday and tomorrow, and you're going to let me love you."

Chapter Eleven

The next day, Jonas left the house at an early hour, and for the rest of the day, he threw himself into his work. The men all appeared happy to have him back at the helm, and he was grateful for their friendship and respect. He was also grateful for the distraction of dealing with the men's work orders and with the minor problems that had cropped up while he'd been away.

Yet even with all the work demanding his attention, he couldn't get Alexa off his mind. Their lovemaking had been just that—love. So sweet and hot and deep that even just thinking about it made his heart turn over, his body long to have her back in his arms.

He'd told her that he'd never expected to want her so much. But if he'd been truly open with her, he would have also told her that he'd never expected to love her so much. And that scared the hell out of Jonas. The words had actually been on the tip of his tongue, but something had prevented him from pushing them past his lips.

Was it because he was afraid of hurting her or losing her?

Hell, Jonas, you're afraid of both. Face the fact. You're a Texas Ranger, and you're brave enough to stare down a bullet if need be. But you're afraid of a blue-eyed woman who melts your heart. Afraid that in the end you won't be man enough to keep her happy.

"Where are you going this late in the evening?"

Jonas recognized Laramie's voice, which came from behind him. Not bothering to glance over his shoulder, he continued to tighten the girth on the saddle.

"Gonna do a little camping tonight." A few minutes ago, he'd slung saddlebags filled with food over the back of his saddle. Now he tied a bedroll and slicker over the bulging bags.

"Camping?" Laramie quizzically repeated the word. "What in the world for? You just got a yen to sleep on the ground and get a backache?"

Even though he felt as glum as a rainy winter day, Jonas forced himself to chuckle. "I suppose. I've decided to take a night, maybe more, and go have a look at the canyon for myself. And while I'm at it, the night air will do me good."

Leaning his arm on the rump of Jonas's horse, the other man stared skeptically at him. "Why don't you just pull a lawn chair outside the barn and sit there for a while? That ought to give you plenty of night air."

"That wouldn't give me a look at the canyon."

With the bedroll safely fastened, Jonas stepped back from his task and looked at the other man. Laramie shook his head.

"You're obsessed about that cut fence, Jonas. And for the life of me, I can't figure out why. Nothing else is gonna happen in the canyon. Trust me. Whoever caused the mischief isn't going to take the trouble to go all the way back into the mountains to do it again."

Jonas wished he could explain the whole

situation to the foreman, but he couldn't. Not until the case was solved or Leo called him back home.

"Maybe not. Just humor me, Laramie. And if you need me for anything, you'll know where to find me."

The other man glanced pointedly toward the house. "Do the folks in the house know you're going to be gone tonight?"

Early this morning, before Jonas had left Alexa at the breakfast table, Frankie had called to say she'd be spending another night away from the ranch. Jonas knew that with her mother gone, Alexa would be expecting him to return to the house right about now. She'd probably planned for him to spend another night in her arms, in her bed. The notion filled him with hungry desire. Yet it also filled him with resolve.

No matter what had happened between the two of them last night, first and foremost, he was here to do a job. And while he was at it, he was going to make Alexa see that trying to make a life with him was the worst thing she could possibly do.

"I left word with Reena. She'll let them know."

He could see questions roiling around in

Laramie's head, but thankfully, the other man didn't ask them. Because right now, Jonas was certainly short on answers.

Later that evening in the house, Alexa passed Sassy on her way to the kitchen.

"Does Reena have dinner ready?" Alexa asked the maid.

The young redhead paused and then stopped her dust mopping. "Yes. She's already left for the day. And she told me to tell you that Jonas wouldn't be back tonight. He had to go do something."

Alexa's heart sank. "Do something? What are you talking about?"

Sassy shrugged. "She didn't explain. Just said he was going to do some horseback riding."

Alexa's brow furrowed into a puzzled frown. Why hadn't he told her he wouldn't be home tonight? He'd known Frankie was going to be away again. All day she'd been planning the evening, dreaming about them spending another night together. She'd believed he'd been doing the same. But evidently, she'd been wrong.

"Don't look so sad, Alexa. You know how cowboys are—sometimes they just have to get on a horse and ride off to who knows where. If they couldn't, it would kill 'em."

A man ought to be able to do what he wants to do the most.

Jonas's words suddenly came to Alexa's mind, and she wondered if his being away this evening had something to do with the rustling case. She had to believe it did. Otherwise, he wouldn't have just gone off without a good reason. And if she was ever going to make him believe that she could deal with his job, she had to trust him, show him that he was dealing with a different woman now and not his ex-wife.

Three days later, Alexa decided that holding on to that resolve was much easier said than done. Jonas had still yet to reappear at the house, and she was thinking about heading down to the stables to question Laramie when he suddenly walked in the back door, with an armload of dirty clothes.

"Jonas!" she exclaimed.

"Hello, ladies."

From her spot at the cabinet counter, Reena nodded a quiet greeting at him. Alexa stood staring at him in stunned fascination.

His face and neck were covered with stubbly beard, while his clothes were all wrinkled and grimy. His hair lay in tumbled disarray across his forehead, while lines of fatigue etched his mouth and eyes. Wherever he'd been, he'd certainly not been living the high life.

"Jonas!" Alexa said again. "Where have you—are you okay?"

"Of course, I'm okay," he replied. Walking over to the mudroom, he opened the door and tossed his dirty clothes into a hamper. When he stepped back into the kitchen, Reena said, "There's fresh coffee, Jonas. Would you like a cup?"

"I could sure use one, but I've got to get a shower first," he told her. "I don't want to stink up your kitchen."

He started out of the room, and Alexa followed promptly on his heels.

"Jonas! You haven't answered me. Where have you been? You've been gone for three days. Reena said you were going out riding and—"

"I did go riding." As they walked down a short hallway, he glanced around him, then lowered his voice so that only she would hear. "I've been out at the canyon near Pickens's land. I camped there, staking out the area. Waiting for something to happen."

Alexa wanted to scream. "And did it?"

"No. Nothing."

"I'm sorry about that. But can you imagine what I've been thinking, feeling? You left without a word to me."

"I told Reena to tell you I'd be gone."

By now they'd reached the stairs, and Alexa had to practically leap up each step to keep up with him. How different, she thought, than the gentle way he'd helped her up the staircase while she'd been pregnant with J.D. Apparently, those considerate days were over, she thought crossly.

"That's hardly the same, Jonas! You've been gone for three days without a word!"

He looked at her, his face unflinching. "That's right, Alexa. Get used to it."

He started to move on up the stairs and away from her, but Alexa's blood was already boiling, and she grabbed him by the arm to prevent his escape.

"Not so fast, Jonas. You're coming with me!"

For a moment she thought he was going to plant his boots on the stairs and remain there like a stubborn mule, but thankfully, he relented, and she quickly led him inside her bedroom and snapped the door shut.

"Where's J.D.?" he asked as he spotted the empty crib.

"As if you care," she flung at him. Then, with a regretful shake of her head, she said, "Forget that I said that. I didn't mean it. And J.D. is with his grandmother. She took him over to the Hondo Valley to see Chloe Sanders—a dear, longtime friend of hers."

"I see."

"No! You don't see! But I do!" She stood before him, her blue eyes shooting sparks at him. "I'm not stupid, Jonas. I might have made some naive choices in the past when it came to men, but that doesn't mean I'm a total idiot now. You're doing all this on purpose. You went out to the canyon to deliberately put distance between us."

Tilting his face toward the ceiling, he sighed. "Alexa, I came here to the Chaparral to find a group of rustlers. I've not done that yet, and my captain is expecting results. One way or the other, if something doesn't happen soon, he's going to axe this thing and call me back to Texas!"

"You were just in Texas," she reasoned. "If he'd had that on his mind, he wouldn't have sent you back to New Mexico."

He leveled an impatient look at her. "All

right, damn it! Maybe he does have plans to give me a few more weeks on the case, but that's beside the point. I need—"

Stepping closer, she placed her palms upon his chest. "You need to convince yourself that you don't care about me or J.D. You need to convince yourself that you don't want us in your life."

As he stared down at her, his lips clamped together with frustration. "I need to catch a band of rustlers the best way that I know how. I also needed to show you just exactly what it would be like to be married to a Ranger. These past few days, they weren't pleasant, were they?"

The fire went out of her eyes as she realized he'd totally misinterpreted her ire. "Jonas," she said softly as her head shook back and forth, "I wasn't upset because you were gone for three days. I had already come to the conclusion that you were doing something about the case. I can wait on you for three days, three months, three years if I have to. But I was hurt because you deliberately avoided telling me your plans."

His nostrils flared, and she could see from the emotions flickering in his eyes that he wasn't nearly as indifferent as he wanted her to think. In fact, she got the feeling that he wanted to pull her into his arms. He was just too stubborn to let himself.

"That's just it, Alexa. Sometimes things like that happen with my job. I have to leave at a moment's notice."

Her hands moved back and forth against his chest. "Like I said, Jonas, I'm not stupid. But I do want to know one thing. Were you lying to me the other night, after we made love, when you told me how much you wanted me?"

He made a garbled noise in his throat, and then, suddenly, his hands were on her shoulders, dragging her close against him.

"You know the answer to that," he muttered.

Alexa opened her mouth to reply, but his mouth quickly put a stop to anything she might have said.

Once again, the time that had separated them had fueled their need for each other. His lips opened roughly over hers, and along with the precious taste of him, she was aware of his beard scratching her cheek and chin, his fingers dipping into the flesh of her shoulders.

While his lips rocked back and forth over

hers, his hands left her shoulders, slid down her back and onto her buttocks.

When he yanked the juncture of her hips up against his bulging arousal, she whimpered with need and slipped her arms around his neck.

Her reaction must have jolted him, reminded him that they were on the verge of making love and that he wasn't about to let it happen again.

Ripping his mouth from hers, he pulled himself away from her. As he sucked in several harsh breaths, his gaze wavered, then dropped to a spot on the floor.

"All right, Alexa. You can see how much I want you. I can't deny that. But we—this can't go on. It *isn't* going to go on! One way or the other, I'm going to be leaving soon. And you'll not be going with me."

Alexa told herself that he really didn't mean what he was saying. That he really didn't want to reject her. Even so, he was rejecting her just the same, and the pain that was quickly settling in her heart was like nothing she'd ever experienced before. It robbed her lungs of air. It twisted her stomach into knots.

Shaking her head, she stared at him in stunned wonder. "You don't deserve to be in my room. And you certainly don't deserve to be in my heart. Please leave. And don't come back until you're man enough to face me with the truth!"

His head jerked at the same time that his chin thrust forward. "What do you mean, the truth?"

"That you love me."

Something flickered in his eyes, and for a second, she thought he was going to reach for her again. But then his face turned to a cool blank, and he turned on his heel and hurried out of the room.

Two days later, Jonas was camped in a rock ravine high above the boxed canyon, a place where he could easily spot anyone who entered or left the area, but that provided him with plenty of cover.

The evening sun was just dipping behind the mountains, and he'd just downed a can of Vienna sausage and a warm beer, when he noticed a movement in the trees several hundred yards below.

Pulling a pair of binoculars from his saddlebag, he jammed them to his face, then cursed under his breath. The rider on the bay horse was Quint. Early this morning, he'd called Alexa's brother and told him where he'd be, just in case the other man needed him, but he'd not expected Quint to ride out here. Jonas could only hope to hell the other man hadn't been observed by anyone on his way.

Ten minutes passed before Quint drew close enough for Jonas to rise from his spot and signal to the man. After that, it took Quint five minutes' time to climb up to Jonas's rocky perch.

"I was beginning to think you'd moved on to another place," Quint said when he finally reached Jonas's hidden nook.

"I wouldn't have let you ride away without signaling," Jonas told him. He gestured to one of the flat rocks he'd been using as a chair. "Have a seat. I'd offer you coffee, but I haven't been building fires. I can't risk the scent or the sight of smoke plumes. But I've got a hot beer left."

"No thanks. I've got a canteen of water on my saddle." Quint settled himself on the rock, then peered down at the canyon below them. "I haven't been out here in years," he said. "I wasn't sure I could still find it."

Taking a seat on the ground, Jonas rested his back against the dirt wall of the ravine and stretched his legs out in front of him. "I didn't know it was here until Pickens showed me. Up until then I'd ridden for days on Chaparral property and missed this. But fifty thousand acres is a lot of ground to cover. Especially alone."

Quint nodded. "I never could figure out why the Rangers didn't send another guy with you to deal with this problem."

"I made my case for help, but it didn't do any good. I'm supposed to do the work of five or ten men."

Quint remained silent for a short spell, then said, "I'm going to be straight with you, Jonas. I wish I'd never agreed to this whole thing—to you coming here to the ranch."

Troubled by this sudden change in Quint's attitude, Jonas stared at him. "Why? Have I let you down? I've tried to keep everything running, and I know I'm not always available to the men, but they're good hands and hardly need me."

Quint quickly waved a dismissive hand at him. "It's not that. The ranch is fine. You've done fine at managing it. And I realize that catching these damn rustlers is important. Who knows when they might start picking up Chaparral cattle along with the Corrientes. None of that is what concerns me right now. It's Alexa. I've never seen my sister so messed up. When I arrived at the ranch house this afternoon, I found her up in her room, crying."

Jonas felt as though the other man had suddenly stabbed him. He didn't want Alexa to cry, to hurt.

"Is something wrong with J.D.?" he asked quickly.

"No. Sassy had him outside." Quint grimaced. "When I questioned her about being upset, she told me that it was only the baby blues and that she would be all right in a few days."

Jonas's heart felt so heavy in his chest, he wasn't sure that he could keep breathing. "You didn't believe her?"

He looked Jonas in the eye. "No. And maybe it's none of my business, but I'm her brother. I'm worried about her. So what happened, Jonas, when you told her about you being a Ranger?"

Jonas's gaze focused on the rocky soil near his feet. "Nothing really. I expected her to be angry. She wasn't."

Quint picked up a handful of gravel and tossed it over the ledge of the canyon. "Hmm.

I guess I was wrong about everything," he said after a stretch of silence. "I thought my sister was in love with you."

Jonas cleared his throat. "Hell, Quint, we both know that I'm not the man for her. She needs someone who is settled. Someone who works from eight to five and takes two weeks' vacation every June."

"You mean, someone boring? If you think she needs that, then you don't know my sister." He shook his head. "I don't know how much she's told you about herself. But I think you ought to know that she's nothing like the fragile woman she appears to be. She's tough. Before Mitch died, she was every inch the cowgirl. She could ride these mountains all day, searching for strays, and when they were found, she could push them out of the brush and rope them. She planned to be nothing but a ranch woman, and she'd worked side by side with our father. She wasn't afraid to get her hands dirty. When she lost Mitch, she might have forgotten she was tough. But it's still there, deep inside her, and if you're trying to test her—"

"Damn it, Quint. I'm not trying to test her! I'm trying to—love her! The best way I know how."

The other man let out a cynical grunt. "You have a funny way of showing it," he said. Then his eyes narrowed shrewdly on Jonas's weary face. "Or maybe you just don't know how to show it at all."

Jonas stared out at the empty canyon. This man could be right, he thought sadly. In spite of being a lawman like his father, maybe he was more like his mother than he wanted to think. Incapable of expressing or giving love to anyone. If that was the case, then all he could think was, *God, help him.*

A week after Alexa told Jonas to leave her room, she was in the little office located just off the den, where she'd been posting checks and filing invoices all morning. Close by, in a separate chair, J.D. was propped in a plastic carrier, his blue eyes trying their best to focus on his mother.

Each time she glanced at J.D., it never failed to lift her heart. Having a son was the richest blessing she'd ever been given, and her heart swelled with such love for him that at times it brought her to emotional tears.

Yet each time she looked at her baby, she was also reminded of Jonas and how he'd helped to bring the tiny boy into the world.

He'd been so gentle and loving, and she'd clung to his cool strength like it was a lifeline in a howling wind.

But now, Alexa didn't know what to think or do. He didn't want her in his life. Or so it appeared. He'd made it painfully clear that he was going back to Texas without her. Where their relationship was concerned, that should be it. Yet Alexa couldn't bear to think that everything they had shared, all she'd hoped for for their future, was over and finished.

Love couldn't be turned on and off like a neon sign, and in spite of not seeing or speaking with him in days, she knew her love for Jonas was still burning brightly.

"Still working?" Frankie rapped her knuckles on the open door, then stepped into the room. "It's time for lunch, and Reena has put out some of your favorite snacks."

Alexa tried to chuckle, but the sound held little humor. "I don't need to eat potato chips."

Frankie clicked her tongue. "I don't know why. You've lost so much weight since you had J.D. Too much."

"Nursing him has pulled me down," Alexa confessed. "But I'm eating plenty."

Frankie leaned over the baby and rubbed her forefinger against his cheek. The baby squirmed and whimpered, and Alexa's mother used that as an excuse to lift him out of the carrier and cuddle him in her arms.

While Frankie cooed at the baby, Alexa gathered her papers together in a neat pile.

Frankie went on with her motherly admonishing. "Well, as far as I'm concerned you've not been getting enough rest either. You've not gotten out of the house since you visited your grandfather. Why don't you call Laurel and go out shopping with her or something? It would do you good."

"Laurel has been putting in fifty-hour weeks at the animal clinic. I doubt she'd be able to take time off." Alexa glanced gratefully at her mother. "But I've gotten most of the work here finished. So I was thinking about going for a ride this afternoon. Would you mind watching J.D. for me for an hour?"

Frankie looked relieved. "I'd be more than happy. Take more than an hour. Stay out as long as you'd like."

After the women finished the simple lunch that Reena had prepared, Alexa walked down to the stables and picked out one of her favorite horses, Dudley. He was black, with four white stockings and a star on his forehead, but most of all, he was affectionate, and Alexa knew she could trust him to carry her safely wherever she wanted to go.

Since the doctor had pronounced her physically fit enough to do whatever she wanted, she'd gone horseback riding on three different occasions. It had felt wonderful getting back to doing something she'd always loved to do. She only wished that Jonas could be riding by her side, that she could look over and see his smile and know that whatever the future brought, they would deal with it together.

But since their confrontation, he'd not even slept in the house, and though her mother had questioned her about his absence, Alexa had not been able to tell her what had really happened with Jonas. Instead, she'd told her that the men were probably out on a roundup, and that he was staying out at the campsite with the rest of the hands. She didn't want the woman knowing that her daughter had made another horrendous mistake and had fallen for a man that didn't want to make a life with her.

Still, she couldn't let it end like this, she thought doggedly. Somehow she had to make Jonas see that he couldn't allow his past to keep ruling his future.

For the next hour, Alexa was so lost in her

miserable thoughts that she didn't realize just how far she'd ridden until glimpses of a county road could be seen through a dense stand of trees between her and the roadway.

Pulling back on the reins, she stopped the horse long enough to glance at her wristwatch and was shocked to see that she'd been gone for two hours. It was high time she returned.

Deciding it would be faster and easier to travel back to the ranch by way of the road, she urged Dudley forward. Once the horse moved from under the canopy of woods and stepped onto the graveled surface, waning sunlight slanted across the lonely pathway and warmed her shoulders.

She nudged the horse into a quick trot. "Okay, Dudley. Let's go home."

Only a quarter of a mile was behind her and her mount when she was alerted to the loud sound of an approaching vehicle. Pulling the horse to a walk, she maneuvered him to a safe spot in the road just as a large truck and trailer rounded the curve in front of her.

"What in the world?" She muttered the question under her breath. Was Ty Pickens leasing mountain land to a sheepherder? If so, it was sort of late in the summer to be moving sheep up to the mountain meadows.

Keeping Dudley at the side of the road, she waited for the big rig to pass. As it did, she peered through the metal slats of the long double-decker trailer.

Cattle were inside! Not sheep. Cattle! With spotted hides and long horns! Corriente cattle?

A cool chill ran down her spine; at the same time, her heart began to pump at a wild rate.

Don't panic, Alexa! They can't be the rustlers. Those are probably some longhorn cattle that Ty Pickens purchased, and they are now being hauled to his ranch. Just keep moving Dudley forward. Don't pause. Don't look back.

The truck moved on up the mountain, and she was about to breathe a sigh of relief when she spotted yet another truck barreling straight toward her. Apparently, the two vehicles were traveling together. And she didn't have time to wonder if this one was hauling cattle, too. As she drew Dudley safely to one side of the road to allow the vehicle to pass, the semi rolled to a stop, and two men wearing sunglasses and baseball caps jumped from the cab.

Sensing she was in trouble, Alexa dug her spurs into Dudley's sides, but the horse had managed to take only two leaps forward when one of the men grabbed the bridle's cheek strap.

Alexa screamed as the other man yanked her from the saddle and began dragging her toward the semi.

"Stop! What are you doing? Who are you?" Alexa yelled the questions at them at the same time she did her best to dig her heels into the loose gravel of the road surface.

"Shut up, lady!" shouted the man who had her in his grasp.

Twisting her head to one side, she bit down hard on the hand that was gripping her arm.

The man yelped and cursed, and then suddenly something whammed her in the face, and everything went black.

Alexa wasn't sure how long she was knocked out. But when she finally managed to open her eyes and look around her, it was apparent that a fairly substantial amount of time had passed. The sun was now down and twilight was descending over the forest.

Evidently they'd simply tossed her from the semi and left her exactly where she'd landed. She was now lying on her stomach, her face partially buried in a bed of pine needles. She had a dull pain in her forehead and down her left cheek, and she knew without being able to see herself that the eye she was looking through was on the verge of swelling completely shut.

Some twenty feet away, four men were gathered at the side of one of the trucks. Their conversation was filled with expletives and brash laughter, which told Alexa they weren't the least bit worried about having an eyewitness on their hands. Probably because they didn't intend to ever let her be a witness.

Beneath the belly of the truck, several yards beyond, she could barely make out the pieces of a portable pipe fence. She could hear the bawling cattle and smell the dust stirred by their hooves and she knew, without much deduction on her part, that the thieves had unloaded the animals for the night.

This was the scenario that Jonas had pictured, she thought sickly. These were the men he'd been trying desperately to catch.

Oh God, what was she going to do to get out of this mess? Her mother knew she'd gone riding, but Alexa hadn't told her where or exactly when to expect her home. To make matters worse, the grooms had been busy with other chores, and Alexa had saddled Dudley herself.

Damn it, Alexa. Forget about not informing the ranch hands of your plans. With you meandering around in a miserable coma, not paying one bit of attention to the trail you were taking, it would be impossible for them to figure out where you are now!

Stupid, Alexa. Very stupid on your part.

Just as she was berating herself, another thought flashed through her frantically whirling brain. Before she'd left the ranch, she'd dropped her cell phone into her shirt pocket. If it was still there, and she could make a call without the men seeing her, she might get out of this mess before they decided to do something unthinkable to her.

Surprised that they'd not bothered to tie her up, Alexa carefully and slowly tried to move her arm and inch her fingers toward the pocket holding the phone without alerting the men that she'd woken.

With excruciating effort, her fingers finally reached the pocket. But the phone was gone, and her hopes were instantly dashed. The instrument had either fallen from her shirt when the men had nabbed her, or they'd taken it away while she'd been unconscious.

So now what? Common sense told her that if she tried to stand and run, they'd tackle her before she got five feet away. No, she was going to have to think of another plan and hope that someone at the ranch would eventually look for her on this section of the property.

Back at the ranch yard, Jonas had just returned from a trip to town and was walking to his office when Laramie approached him with rapid strides.

Pausing, Jonas waited for the other man to reach him. "Hey, Laramie. What's up? Something wrong?"

"I'm not sure, Jonas. One of the grooms told me that Alexa rode out on Dudley earlier this afternoon, and she's not returned. I called the house and talked to Frankie a couple of hours ago, and at that time she didn't seem all that alarmed. She said that she told Alexa to ride as long as she wanted. But after it started growing dark and late, the woman called me back, and she's practically hysterical with worry."

Jonas was certain his blood had suddenly turned to ice. "Did Frankie know where

Alexa was going to ride? What direction she took?"

"I asked her that," Laramie replied. "She didn't know. But she did say that Alexa took a cell phone with her and that there's no answer when she tries calling it."

"Damn it all!" Jonas muttered. "Well, the phone doesn't mean that something has happened to her. She could have ridden into a dead zone." He turned and began striding quickly toward the horse barn. "Gather the men, Laramie. I'm going to saddle up and ride out."

"Where do you want us to look?"

Jonas groaned with utter despair. "Since we have nothing to go on, look anywhere and everywhere!"

Five minutes later, Jonas had strapped on his weapon, saddled one of the fastest horses from the work pen and loped out of the ranch yard.

For the next few minutes, the big mare ate up the rough ground as Jonas allowed her to pick her own path through the brush and trees. He didn't know how far they'd traveled before it dawned on him that he was riding blindly, without any sense of direction. At the same time, he frantically realized there was no set direction for him to take. He had nothing to go on but his gut instincts.

Find her. Find her. Before something happens, find her!

Over and over the mantra screamed in his head, until finally he pulled the mare to a halt and looked around him. He'd unconsciously ridden along the same damn path he'd taken for several days now. He was headed to the canyon, and he knew Alexa wouldn't be there.

He'd warned her several times not to ride to Pickens's border fence, and she'd promised she wouldn't. He'd taken her at her word and dismissed the idea that she would ever go against his wishes. She was not an idiot. Not one to do risky or stupid things.

Except fall in love with you, Jonas. That was purely stupid on her part. She should have known just how worthless and uncaring you were as a husband. You tried to warn her. But she'd not listened.

Had she also not listened to him about riding toward the Pickens ranch? Had she ended up near the old mining road?

Releasing a choked groan, he dug his heels into the mare's sides and steered the animal toward the boxed canyon.

* * *

"What are we gonna do with her?" one of the men asked.

Alexa, who was now sitting propped against a wheel of one of the trucks, her hands bound behind her with a leather shoelace, covertly studied the four men. The one who'd just spoken appeared more nervous than the other three. Every few minutes he lit a cigarette and paced around the small fire that the men had built to ward off the chill of the evening.

"Relax, Randy, and quit worrying about the chick," the tallest guy of the bunch said. "We'll deal with her later."

From what Alexa could tell, this tall man was the boss of sorts. At least, he was giving most of the orders, she decided, and the others were following them.

"We'd better leave her here," said the one called Randy. "Rustlin' charges ain't nothin' compared to what they'd do to us for kidnappin'. My plans don't include rottin' in a penitentiary!"

"Oh hell, Randy, use that pea brain of yours a little," the tall one barked back. "If we get caught, it ain't gonna make any difference what we're charged with. We'll be making license plates till we die."

The youngest man, who wore wire-rimmed glasses and a Texas A&M sweatshirt, grinned and chuckled. "If that's the case, then we might as well take the chick with us. Might be fun to have her on the trip. She's pretty." He glanced toward Alexa and grinned again. "Or she would have been if Cecil hadn't punched her in the face."

Alexa shivered with revulsion. She had no idea how long the men planned to stay here in the canyon. Long enough, she supposed, for the cattle to have a little grass and water while the men waited for their contacts. From what she could gather from their sporadic conversation, more men would eventually arrive at the canyon to haul the cattle on the last leg of their journey. In Texas, the herd would be taken to a certain place where the cattle could be tagged, then sold as legal livestock.

So far, since they'd discovered she was conscious, none of them had roughed her up. The youngest one had offered her a drink from his beer can and a candy bar. She'd refused both. Now they were mostly ignoring her and discussing her fate as if she wasn't sitting within earshot.

"The bitch bit me." Cecil sullenly defended his actions. "She deserved to be whacked."

"Maybe you deserve a whacking, too, you damned coward!" the youngest man shot back at him.

Cecil got up and started toward the younger man, but the tall man ordered him back, with a pointed finger.

"Cool it, damn it! Both of you," the tall man shouted. "And let me think about what to do with the woman. Right now, I'm not so sure takin' her along is a grand idea. If we take her into Texas, the Rangers will be on our asses and quick."

"I ain't scared of no Rangers," the youngest guy bragged. "But I don't want to kill her. I wouldn't cotton to killin' no woman. I don't care what you say about those license plates!"

Oh God, her baby! Would she ever see her son again? What would happen to all the plans she had for him? Who would love him, mother him? And Jonas. He lived and burned in her heart. Were all her hopes and plans for them to be together going to end right here at this boxed canyon?

The questions choked her, and she bit down hard on her lip to keep from sobbing out loud. If Jonas was in this situation, he wouldn't panic, she firmly scolded herself. He'd try to think of some way to escape, some way to distract these thugs.

She was watching their every move, making every effort to conceal the movements of her hands as she raked the tangled shoestring up and down against the metal when Dudley suddenly let out a loud whinny and began to dance back and forth against the tied reins.

Hope surged. Another horse had to be around. She was sure of that. But was there a rider on it? Or was it just a herd of the Chaparral mares that roamed loose with their young colts?

Oh, God, she desperately prayed, *let it be Jonas!*

Alerted by the horse's sudden behavior, the tall man, the one Alexa had mentally tagged the boss, jerked his head around in all directions, while the other three attempted to peer into the darkened woods.

"What's the matter with that damned horse?" the one called Cecil mumbled.

"The cattle may have gotten loose," the tall man said and motioned for the other men to follow him. "We'd better go take a look."

All the men marched after the tall man, except the youngest man, the ladies' man.

But none of the others seemed to notice he'd lagged behind.

Alexa shivered inwardly as he sauntered over to where she sat, then squatted on his heels in front of her.

"Hey, pretty missy, how about me and you gettin' out of here and goin' for a little walk? I'm not like Cecil. I won't hurt ya."

It was all Alexa could do to keep from spitting in his face, but she somehow managed to bite back the urge. This young Romeo might afford her the only chance she had to escape, and no matter how repulsive he was, she had to take it.

"I do need to stretch my legs," she admitted.

Her jaw hurt when she talked, and she wondered if it was broken. But a fractured jaw would be the least of her worries if these men carted her off in their cattle truck.

With a lecherous grin, he reached for her arm. As he pulled her to her feet, she got the sickening whiff of tobacco juice mixed with bologna.

"Now that's a good girl," he crooned.

Tugging her to her feet, he led her into the woods and away from the other men and the cattle. The moment they were out of sight, he slipped his arm around her shoulders, and Alexa very nearly froze with revulsion and fear. Yet somewhere deep within, she heard Jonas telling her to use her head and instincts to survive.

Swallowing at the bile rising in her throat, she addressed her captor in the sweetest voice she could summon. "Shouldn't you untie my wrists? I can't show you a good time like this."

Chuckling, he lowered his mouth close to her ear. "Aw now you're tryin' to be sneaky with ole Josh here, ain't you? You wanta jump me and get away."

"I'm a helpless female. I couldn't match your strength. But maybe you don't like a woman's hands on you," she added with feigned coyness.

The last goading got him, and hope whipped through her as he fished a knife from his jeans pocket, then spun her around and began to saw at the shoestring binding her wrists.

"We ain't got much time," he muttered. "You—"

"Better be scared of Texas Rangers! Because this one has just come after you!"

She heard Jonas's low, guttural warning,

and a split second later her captor muttered a filthy expletive. The one word was all the young thief managed to get out before Jonas whacked him over the head with the butt of his pistol and he crumpled to the ground.

Sobbing, her legs threating to collapse, Alexa whirled and flung herself against Jonas.

"Jonas! Oh, God, Jonas!"

Snatching her into the tight circle of his arms, he quickly whispered against her ear. "Sh. Don't let them hear you. Just tell me— are you all right? Have they hurt you?"

Even as he asked the questions, his lips were pressing frantic kisses across her forehead, on her hair and along her cheek.

"Just my face," she answered. "I—"

Easing her back, he held up a penlight, then cursed as he spotted the swollen black eye and cheek. "God, these guys are going to pay, Alexa! But right now I just thank God I found you!"

Jerking the remaining bits of shoestring away from her hands, he helped her over to a large rock and ordered her to hunker down behind it. "Stay here! Don't move. Don't make a sound until I come after you! Understand?"

She clutched the front of his shirt, and he paused long enough to cradle her face in his hands.

"Be careful, Jonas! I don't want to lose you now! Ever!"

Groaning, he brought his lips down on hers in a hard, hungry promise. "You're not going to lose me, sweetheart."

He pulled away from her, and as he slipped off into the darkness in search of the dangerous men, Alexa wanted to beg him not to go. Now that she was free, the two of them could slip off into the darkness and make it back to the safety of the ranch.

But this was his job, she reminded herself. It was what he wanted and needed to do. No matter how much she feared for his safety, she couldn't try to pull him away from his work.

From somewhere near the parked semi-trucks, she could hear the men shouting, calling out for her and her fallen suitor, and then behind her, another horse, the one she figured Jonas had quietly ridden up on, nickered loudly.

A silence ensued for several minutes after that, and Alexa's stomach remained clenched in fearful knots. Had something happened to

Jonas? Had these thugs jumped him? Taken his weapon away?

Even with the Romeo knocked unconscious, Jonas was still outnumbered: he had three men to deal with on his own! Oh God, it didn't matter about her own life now, she thought. Without him, she could never be whole.

Time seemed suspended as she waited; then finally she heard Jonas shouting and then metal clanking. The horses continued to call to each other, and then there was more clanging and banging of metal.

Uncertainty and fear urged her to move from behind the rock and search for Jonas, while at the same time she fought to obey his order to stay put.

Finally the soft call of his voice flooded her heart with joyous relief.

"Over here, Alexa. It's okay. It's all over."

Sobbing, she ran to him and the safety of his arms.

Minutes later, after Jonas had revived the youngest thief and thrown him into one of the cattle trailers with the rest of the rustlers, he helped Alexa into the truck's cab and then drove them all back to the ranch house.

During the trip, Jonas made several calls, including one to the local sheriff to report the crime and request his help. He also notified Quint that Alexa was safe so, in turn, he could tell Frankie and everyone at the ranch the good news.

Each time he hung up the phone, Alexa looked for a chance to speak with him. There was so much she wanted to say, much she needed to hear. But this case had involved several different agencies, and he was quickly trying to alert them all as to what had just taken place. By the time he ended his conversation with Leo, his captain, they had reached the ranch, and she could see Quint and her mother standing in the middle of the ranch yard, waiting to greet them.

As soon as Jonas brought the big rig to a stop, Quint jerked open the door and helped Alexa to the ground. After he hugged his sister tightly and kissed her several times, Frankie snatched her into her arms.

"J.D.?" Alexa asked as soon as she could speak. "Where is he? Is he okay?"

"He's fine. Sassy has him in the nursery," Frankie assured her. Then, with tears streaming down her cheeks, she used both hands to smooth Alexa's hair away from her face.

"Alexa! My God, your eye and cheek! I was afraid you'd fallen and broken your neck! I didn't know anything about rustlers until a few minutes ago!"

Alexa shook her head with regret. She'd caused so many people so much worry. But there was a silver lining to the whole incident. At least, the rustlers had been found and caught.

"I'm sorry, Mother. Jonas warned me about riding too far away from the ranch. But I wasn't paying close attention, and before I realized it, I was near the old county road on the other side of Chaparral property. I had just decided to follow the road back to the ranch when those—those men jumped out of their truck and nabbed me."

Openly sobbing with relief, Frankie clung to Alexa for long moments before she finally eased her daughter out of her arms and shot her a reproving look. "You've been keeping secrets, young lady—but I'm hardly the person to scold you over that," she said, with a tearful smile. "Besides, that part doesn't matter now. You're safe. Thank God!"

"You're damn right it doesn't matter," Quint exclaimed as he jerked his sister back into the safe circle of his arms. "Jonas saved

Alexa and rounded up a bunch of thieving thugs while he was at it. What's there to fuss about?"

"Jonas. Where is he?" Alexa twisted her head in search of him.

Quint jerked his thumb back over his shoulder. "While Mom had you in her clutches, the sheriff and deputies arrived. He's with them."

Stepping out of her brother's embrace, Alexa glanced over to see a group of official county vehicles parked near one of the cattle pens. At the front of a four-wheel-drive truck, Jonas was standing with the county sheriff and two other lawmen. A map was laid out on the hood, and Jonas was deep in conversation as he pointed out areas and gave directions. For now, he'd forgotten all about Alexa.

Frankie spoke up. "Come along, darling. I know you want to see J.D., and you need a shower and food. I'm going to call Dr. Donovan and have her come out and check your eye and cheek."

Taking her by the arm, Frankie urged her daughter toward the house. Quint excused himself and headed off to join Jonas and the lawmen to offer his help.

"My eye and cheek will be okay, Mom.

There's no need to call Bridget all the way out here. I'll put an ice pack on my face."

"Nonsense. Making house calls is her specialty. And I want to make sure there's no damage that might need more serious medical attention."

Alexa was too weary to waste any more breath arguing with her mother about it. Frankie would overly compensate Dr. Donovan for her trouble. Right now Alexa's major concern was getting her baby back in her arms and finding a chance to speak privately with Jonas.

He'd said she wasn't going to lose him. But had he been talking about the future? Or had he said those words just to calm her while they'd been in a difficult situation? Obviously he'd been desperate to rescue her. But that was his job, to rescue anyone whose life was in danger.

Hours passed before Alexa finally got the opportunity to see Jonas again. She was lying on a small couch in the atrium, waiting and watching for his return, when he finally stepped through the door.

Jumping to her feet, she switched on a lamp and startled him in the process.

"Alexa!" he exclaimed with dismay. "What are you doing out here?"

Moving across the room to him, she could see weariness etched upon his rugged features, and she ached to hold him in her arms, to soothe away every worry from his heart.

She came to a stop within inches of him, and suddenly her heart was bursting to tell him all that she was feeling, fearing, wanting. "I couldn't sleep," she admitted. "Not until I had a chance to—see you."

His eyes met hers and then, with a great groan, he swept her into his arms and buried his face in her neck. "Oh, darling. Oh, Alexa, my love."

Slipping her arms around his waist, she pressed her face against his warm chest.

"Jonas, oh, Jonas," she mumbled sorrowfully. "When I told you that you didn't deserve to be in my bedroom or my heart, I didn't mean it. Forgive me. All these days I've been wondering what to do—how to convince you not to throw my love away. I won't let you!"

Wrapping his arms tightly around her, he held her so close that she realized he never meant to let her go.

"Don't ask me to forgive you, Alexa.

There's nothing to forgive. I've acted like a crazy man. And I don't deserve your love." His face was pressed against her hair, and her thick locks muffled his next words. "Tonight, when Laramie told me you were missing, I felt the world being jerked from under my feet. If something had happened to you—"

With his hands on her shoulders, he eased her away from him just enough to see her face. As he took in the bruises and swelling, the horror of what she must have gone through brought a sting of tears to his eyes.

"I don't want to live without you, Alexa," he said simply. "I love you. I've loved you almost from the very start. But every time the mere thought of the word entered my mind, I tried to push it out. These past few days I've been trying to convince myself that I could go back to Texas without you. But even before the rustlers grabbed you, I was coming to the conclusion that I couldn't just walk away from you. Do you still love me, Alexa? Do you still want us to be a family?"

Joy settled in the bottom of her heart, then swelled upward and outward, until her whole being felt as if it were riding a golden cloud.

"Jonas, I love you, need you! J.D. needs you to be his father. And I want you to be the father of any other children I'm blessed to have. Does that answer your question?"

"My job will always—"

"Make you extra special to me." As she finished the sentence for him, her hands came up to frame his doubtful face. "Jonas, tonight I saw firsthand just how important your job is, how much it's a part of you. I'd never want to separate the two of you. I understand that after we're married, there will be times we can't be together. But as long as I know you'll be coming home to me, that's all that matters."

Swallowing hard, he rested his forehead against hers. "Your brother accused me of not knowing how to show my love to another person, and I've had to admit to myself that he was right."

"Oh, Jonas, that's—"

Shaking his head, he said quickly, "No, wait, Alexa. Hear me out. Quint was right. Now that I've looked back on my life, I can see that things were different—so very different—for me than they've been for you. My parents weren't happy people. My mother— I can't remember hugs or kisses from her. I can't remember a time I saw her touch my father with affection. I can't recall her offering him praise the way that you've praised me. I guess I never learned to express my feelings, and when I tried to with Celia, I must have come off as halfhearted. I don't know. I just know that I'm not going to make the same mistakes with you as I did with her. I'm not going to lose you, Alexa. Not now or ever."

Rising up on her tiptoes, she rubbed her lips against his. "The rustling case is closed on this end. When do we pack to go to Texas?"

Laughing softly, he glanced around him. "Where is our son? Asleep?"

Alexa's arms slipped around his neck as she pulled him even closer. "Asleep. With his grandmother," she whispered. "Somehow I think she understood that I needed to be with you tonight."

He brought his lips next to hers. "Hmm. Remind me to tell her what a good mother-in-law she's going to be."

Epilogue

Almost a year later, deep in the heart of Texas, on the Redman Ranch, family and friends crowded around the chairs and tables erected on the back lawn, beneath the limbs of a giant, spreading live oak.

Because Abe had refused to board a jet, Quint had driven him and Frankie the several hundred miles to San Antonio to be here for the occasion. Quint and Alexa's half brothers, Mac and Ripp, along with their young families, had also driven up for the party. And Jonas had been pleasantly surprised when his older sister, Bethany, had arrived with their younger brother, Bart, in tow.

A few minutes ago, after the barbecue dinner had been downed, Alexa had placed a small birthday cake in front of J.D. The black-haired toddler had stared at the object for long moments before he'd finally squealed with delight, then smashed the sweet concoction between his two little hands. He'd smeared more cake on his face and shirt than what he'd managed to get into his mouth, but he'd had a blast doing it. So much so that he'd cried when Alexa had finally taken the cake away and cleaned him.

But his fussing quickly ended when his daddy sat him down on the patio, among a pile of brightly wrapped presents. For the next few minutes, as she and Jonas watched with loving eyes as their son dug into his first birthday toys, Alexa was reminded that the past year had been full of pleasant surprises, new adventures and, most of all, love. Her life with Jonas and their son was all that she'd imagined and more.

In the end, the rustling thieves who'd nabbed Alexa squealed on the ringleaders in order to lessen their sentences. Jonas's suspicions about a Pickens ranch hand being involved in the crime had also been correct. That man had been arrested for aiding and abetting and had been convicted along with the rest. Jonas had been commended by his peers for his valiant effort, and since then he'd moved on to other cases.

Alexa never failed to encourage her husband, and in turn, Jonas made sure he showed her and their son how very much he loved them. And she'd taken over the management of his ranch, which was flourishing.

"My boy is already walking strong," Abe said proudly to Alexa as she served her grandfather a cup of strong coffee. "He'll be riding by himself in no time. Jonas will see to that. And so will I." He glanced slyly up at her. "So when are you and Jonas gonna have another one? Soon, I hope. I ain't getting no younger, you know. I want to be around to see it get here. Your granny and me never could have another child after Lewis. Now it's up to you and Quint to keep the family goin'."

Smiling secretively, she said, "We're working on it, Gramps."

"Well, work a little faster," he said with a snort.

She propped a hip on the arm of his wooden lawn chair and slipped her arm across the back of her grandfather's shoulders. Abe had never been one to step off Apache Wells unless he had to. But J.D. had become the apple of his great-grandfather's eye, and Alexa hadn't had to do much cajoling to get the old man to come to Texas for the baby's birthday celebration.

Since he'd been here, Jonas had made a special effort to show Abe around the ranch and ask his opinion on everything from cattle to fence building. Seeing the fond affection that had grown between the two men filled her with more happiness than she could express.

"Gramps, I wish you'd decide to stay here with us for a while longer. At least another month. We have plenty of room for you."

He patted her hand. "It sounds temptin', honey. I like this hot, steamy air. Makes a man sweat and feel good. Maybe I'll come back later and stay awhile."

"Why not stay now? Frankie has a new man in her life, and he's keeping her happily occupied. And Quint's busy—he's almost got the new ranch built. He doesn't have to have you around."

The old man chuckled as he gazed across the lawn to where Quint was relaxing in a lawn chair, sharing a beer with Jonas.

"Quint don't know it yet, but I'm about to have a surprise for him."

Alexa looked curiously down at her grandfather. "What sort of surprise? Gramps, you're not still harping on opening the Golden Spur, are you?"

Smiling slyly, Abe stroked his chin whiskers with a thumb and forefinger. "Could be. Could be that and a whole lot more."

Alexa didn't ask her grandfather for details. She'd learned long ago that he didn't give away any thought in his head until he was good and ready to let it loose. Yet later that night, as she sat in front of her bedroom dressing table brushing her hair, her grandfather's comment continued to drift through her mind.

"You're looking awfully preoccupied." Coming up behind her, Jonas settled his hands on the tops of her shoulders. "If I were a jealous husband, I'd say you had another man on your mind."

Smiling coyly, she put the brush aside and reached up to cover both his hands with hers. "Actually, I was thinking about another man," she admitted. "Gramps, to be exact."

Jonas chuckled. "Oh. What has the old codger done now?" he asked. Then, his expression serious, he added, "He is feeling all right, isn't he? He seemed fine when he retired to his bedroom a few minutes ago."

"Don't worry. He's feeling great. It was something he said earlier today at the party that I'm wondering about. He implied that he had a surprise in store for Quint. But he didn't say what. I'm thinking he's up to something outrageous—probably something connected to the Golden Spur." Twisting her head around, she looked up at her husband. "I wish he'd get that old mine out of his head once and for all."

His eyelids dropping to two sexy slits, Jonas pulled her up from the dressing bench and into his arms. The thin satin of her nightgown heated as his hands began to roam across her back and down to her hips. His touch never failed to thrill her, and she pressed her body closer.

"Quint's a big boy. He can take care of himself," he whispered huskily. "Right now I want your mind on other things. Like you and me. And this."

As his head sank toward hers, a dreamy look turned her eyes smoky-blue. "Gramps wanted to know when we're going to have another baby. I didn't tell him that I was already expecting our child. I wanted to give you, my love, the gift of telling him and everyone the news."

"You and our babies. I couldn't be more blessed," he murmured.

As his lips settled hungrily over hers, Alexa wrapped her arms around his neck and let his kiss carry her away to that special place, where her only thought was loving this man for the rest of her life.

* * * * *

WESTERN WP PROMISES

YES! Please send me **The Western Promises Collection** in Larger Print. This collection begins with 3 FREE books and 2 FREE gifts (gifts valued at approx. $14.00 retail) in the first shipment, along with the other first 4 books from the collection! If I do not cancel, I will receive 8 monthly shipments until I have the entire 51-book Western Promises collection. I will receive 2 or 3 FREE books in each shipment and I will pay just $4.99 US/ $5.89 CDN for each of the other four books in each shipment, plus $2.99 for shipping and handling per shipment. *If I decide to keep the entire collection, I'll have paid for only 32 books, because 19 books are FREE! I understand that accepting the 3 free books and gifts places me under no obligation to buy anything. I can always return a shipment and cancel at any time. My free books and gifts are mine to keep no matter what I decide.

272 HCN 3070 472 HCN 3070

Name _____ (PLEASE PRINT) _____

Address _____ Apt. # _____

City _____ State/Prov. _____ Zip/Postal Code _____

Signature (if under 18, a parent or guardian must sign)

Mail to the **Reader Service:**
IN U.S.A.: P.O. Box 1867, Buffalo, NY 14240-1867
IN CANADA: P.O. Box 609, Fort Erie, Ontario L2A 5X3

WPBPA16R

REQUEST YOUR FREE BOOKS!
2 FREE NOVELS PLUS 2 FREE GIFTS!

HARLEQUIN®

Western Romance

ROMANCE THE ALL-AMERICAN WAY!

READERSERVICE.COM

Manage your account online!

- Review your order history
- Manage your payments
- Update your address

> **We've designed the
> Reader Service website
> just for you.**

Enjoy all the features!

- Discover new series available to you, and read excerpts from any series.
- Respond to mailings and special monthly offers.
- Connect with favorite authors at the blog.
- Browse the Bonus Bucks catalog and online-only exculsives.
- Share your feedback.

Visit us at:
ReaderService.com